"You're pregnant."

Caleb's heart started to pound as he said the words. Joy and fear assailed him at once. He'd always dreamed of having a child. But not now...not with killers after him.

He could see the deep vulnerability in Shannon's shadowed eyes. She hugged herself, then rubbed her arms as if she were freezing. "I want to know what you're going to do," she said.

There was no doubt in his mind. "I'm going to be the best father a child can have."

"So you're planning on being there for him or her?" Her tone was icy. "Alive?"

So that was where this was going, he thought. His undercover work. He looked at her and tried to talk, but he didn't know how to tell her he loved her and that he didn't want her taken away from him. The baby, either.

"It's not me I'm worried about," he finally said. "It's you."

Her eyes widened.

"If the men I'm after find out about you and the... baby, then you'll be their first target."

Dear Harlequin Intrigue Reader,

All the evidence is in! And it would be a crime if you didn't "Get Caught Reading" this May. So follow the clues to your favorite bookstore to pick up some great tips.

This month Harlequin Intrigue has the distinguished privilege of launching a *brand-new* Harlequin continuity series with three of our top authors. TRUEBLOOD, TEXAS is a story of family and fortitude set in the great Lone Star state. We are pleased to give you your first look into this compelling drama with *Someone's Baby* by Dani Sinclair. Look for books from B.J. Daniels and Joanna Wayne to follow in the months ahead. You won't want to miss even a single detail!

Your favorite feline detective is back in *Familiar Lullaby* by Caroline Burnes. This time, Familiar's ladylove Clotilde gets in on the action when a baby is left on a high-society doorstep. Join a feisty reporter and a sexy detective as they search for the solution and find true love in this FEAR FAMILIAR mystery.

Our TOP SECRET BABIES promotion concludes this month with *Conception Cover-Up* by Karen Lawton Barrett. See how far a father will go to protect his unborn child and the woman he loves. Finally, Carly Bishop takes you out West for a showdown under a blaze of bullets in *No One But You*, the last installment in her LOVERS UNDER COVER trilogy.

So treat yourself to all four. You won't be disappointed.

Sincerely,

Denise O'Sullivan
Associate Senior Editor
Harlequin Intrigue

CONCEPTION COVER-UP

KAREN LAWTON BARRETT

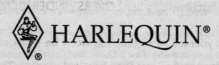

HARLEQUIN®

TORONTO • NEW YORK • LONDON
AMSTERDAM • PARIS • SYDNEY • HAMBURG
STOCKHOLM • ATHENS • TOKYO • MILAN • MADRID
PRAGUE • WARSAW • BUDAPEST • AUCKLAND

ISBN 0-373-22615-2

CONCEPTION COVER-UP

Copyright © 2001 by Karen Lawton Barrett

This edition published by arrangement with Harlequin Books S.A.

® and TM are trademarks of the publisher. Trademarks indicated with ® are registered in the United States Patent and Trademark Office, the Canadian Trade Marks Office and in other countries.

Visit us at www.eHarlequin.com

Printed in U.S.A.

ABOUT THE AUTHOR

Karen Lawton Barrett was raised in a small town in
central California, where one of her elementary school
teachers once wrote on a report card, "Karen day-
dreams too much." These days she uses her active
imagination to create romantic suspense stories.

Books by Karen Lawton Barrett

HARLEQUIN INTRIGUE
560—HERS TO REMEMBER
615—CONCEPTION COVER-UP

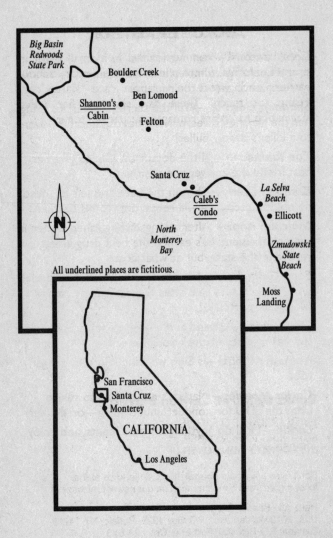

Big Basin
Redwoods
State Park

Boulder Creek

Ben Lomond

Shannon's
Cabin

Felton

Santa Cruz

La Selva
Beach

Caleb's
Condo

Ellicott

North
Monterey
Bay

Zmudowski
State
Beach

All underlined places are fictitious.

Moss
Landing

San Francisco
Santa Cruz
Monterey

CALIFORNIA

Los Angeles

CAST OF CHARACTERS

Caleb Carlisle—Running for his life from vicious drug dealers, he stumbles into the arms of a woman whose past shadows their future.

Shannon Garrett—Will the secret she carries bring her the life she craves, or will she lose another lover to a killer's deadly bullet?

Zoe Yamana—Will the doctor be able to give her best friend the answer she desires?

Brandon Everly—Shot in the back and left for dead, he holds a secret he will reveal only to his partner.

Malcolm Knox—After a long, distinguished career in law enforcement, he's earned the best drug arrest record in the state, but at what cost?

Sean Gallagher—He's been in charge of the Special Drug Unit for the past fifteen years. Has the stress finally gotten to him?

Sid Muñoz—A friend and fellow agent, he ends up in the wrong place at the wrong time.

Marissa Muñoz—Is Sid's wife and family in danger, too?

Carlos Morales—Marissa's cousin had to resign from the SDU for conduct unbecoming—or did he?

Larkin—He'll do anything his boss wants, and enjoy doing it.

To my darling Duffy and wonderful Phillip,
who bring me love and joy.

To Cherry, for her fearless and unstinting support.

And to the ladies of the BICC, for a terrific ride.

I thank you all.

Chapter One

Branches scraped the side of his four-wheel-drive truck with a sound like fingernails on a blackboard as Caleb Carlisle negotiated the turn onto the sorry excuse for a road that led to the Driscoe brothers' compound. Ancient redwood trees spread their branches over the mud-and-gravel lane, darkening the already gloomy day. A distant rumble of thunder warned of a coming storm.

"I sure hope this rain holds off for a while," he said to his partner, Brandon Everly, who lounged in the passenger seat. Brandon's demeanor was deceptive. They both knew how important this meeting was.

As the road rose sharply, Caleb downshifted. Thunder growled again, closer this time. He accelerated over the last hump and drove into the compound.

Brandon reached behind the seat and grabbed the two backpacks that held the quarter million in cash for the supposed exchange. He handed one to Caleb. "Ready?"

Caleb nodded. Adrenaline pulsed in his veins. The Driscoes had been selling cocaine to the local teenagers like candy. It had taken months of undercover work to get to this point. Now all they needed was the identity of the brothers' superior, the man who could lead them to their international connection. But whether or not they gave up their boss, the Driscoes were going down. Today.

Caleb and Brandon exited the vehicle and headed for the ramshackle barn that housed one of the most efficient cocaine-distribution centers in the state.

Jim Driscoe walked out of the building. Big and beefy, Jim stopped about twenty feet from them, chewing on a toothpick and studying them with shadowed eyes. His brothers followed him out, flanking him. Short fat J.P. stood with his thumbs hooked in his belt. Thin wiry Henry moved restlessly. None of them said a word.

A prickle crawled up Caleb's spine. Something had gone wrong, he knew it. That sixth sense had saved his butt many times before, and he wasn't about to question it now.

Caleb grinned over his foreboding. "What's goin' on, guys? We waitin' for Larkin?" That weasel, the fourth in this little group of thugs, was always slinking around. His absence made Caleb uneasy.

A flash of lightning eerily lit the brothers' unpleasant faces. A loud clap of thunder followed.

Caleb looked up at the sky. "Big storm comin'." He glanced at the brothers. "Let's go inside. We brought you some goodies."

He took a couple of steps forward, but the brothers didn't move.

Jim pulled out a handgun. "You ain't goin' nowhere, pig."

His younger brothers shifted their positions, cutting off Caleb and Brandon's access to the truck.

"What's up, man?" Brandon asked, using his jittery cokehead voice. "We brought you cash, and you pull a gun on us? I thought we were partners, man."

A vicious look came to Jim's face, and he raised his gun. "We ain't partners with no cops."

Caleb threw his bag in Jim's face at the same time Brandon threw his at Henry. Before J.P. could even react, they pulled out their weapons and dove for cover. Within seconds the Driscoes opened fire.

There was a flash of lightning, then another. Thunder almost drowned out the sound of gunfire. And then the sky let loose, pouring down buckets of rain.

Caleb took a quick visual inventory of the situation. They were outnumbered and outflanked by Jim and his brothers.

Jim barked orders at J.P. "Henry and I will take care of them. You get Larkin, then stay by that truck. Don't let those pigs near it. And tell Larkin to call Mick *now*."

Registering the new name just added to the mix, Caleb looked at his partner. They had a choice: Go up the mountain or down. Brandon gestured up. So up they went.

The storm didn't let up as they struggled through the overgrown ferns and bushes that covered the forest floor. They could hear Jim and Henry crashing through the undergrowth close behind them. The dense foliage and heavy rain didn't make it any easier for the brothers, either.

Caleb stopped under a huge redwood for a moment to monitor the drug dealers' progress. Jim and Henry were climbing slowly but steadily up the hill.

He resumed his trek, increasing his speed to catch

up with his partner. They couldn't carry on this pace forever. They had to find a way to take out Jim and Henry, then go back for the others.

Reaching a rushing stream, Caleb stopped Brandon. "This isn't getting us anywhere. Maybe we can circle around and get a jump on them."

Brandon wiped rain out of his eyes. "You take that side of the stream. I'll take this side."

Caleb jumped over the water, then began to circle back. In the silence that followed a clap of thunder, he could hear movement in the bushes not far from where he stood. He stayed absolutely still. Then he caught a glimpse of red plaid—Henry's shirt. When he couldn't see Jim anywhere, he realized the brothers had split up.

He waited behind a huge redwood until Henry came nearer, then called out, "That's far enough, Henry. Drop your gun."

Henry shot toward the tree. One went wide. The second splattered mud on his boots.

Another shot and bark splintered inches from Caleb's face. That was close, he thought. Too close.

Blinking to clear his eyes of the pouring rain, Caleb raised his own weapon. He could hear the rustle of foliage.

"Come on, Henry, you know you aren't going to get away with this," Caleb said, keeping his tone friendly. "Why don't you just put down the gun?"

"I'm doin' nothin' of the kind, cop!" He charged toward the tree, firing madly.

Caleb fired his gun, too, till he heard a grunt.

"Damn you, you hit my leg!" Henry cried.

Caleb stayed where he was. Jim's youngest brother wasn't the brightest guy in the world, but he might be smart enough to fake an injury. Even as the thought struck Caleb, Henry emptied his pistol in the direction of the tree.

A hot sharp pain seared Caleb's upper arm, and he grabbed it with his free hand. One of the bullets had ricocheted. He suspected it was only a graze, but his shooting arm now hurt like hell.

Another shot rang out, and Caleb dropped to a crouch. It hadn't come from Henry... Had Larkin finally decided to join them? He listened intently for movement, but all he could hear was the rain.

"Hey, partner, did we get him?" Brandon's voice sounded from across the stream.

Caleb ventured a look and saw Henry on the ground, very still, blood pooling from a wound in his chest. "Looks like," Caleb yelled back.

"What about Jim?"

Caleb had no idea where Jim was. Then he heard a rumble, deeper than thunder, and the ground began to shake. An earthquake? Several large rocks tumbled by and the ground shook harder. He looked up the mountain.

"Landslide, Bran! Landslide!" Caleb ran to the right as fast as he could. Who knew how wide a swath the slide would cut?

Rain poured, thunder boomed and the mountainside came down faster and faster. Falling rocks struck him as he ran. His arm was on fire, but he knew he had to keep going. He slipped in the mud, once, twice, then got up and ran some more, not daring to stop, rocks and water rushing past him. One of the rocks struck his head and he saw stars. Then there was only blackness.

CALEB AWOKE to a steady rain. The ground beneath him was hard and rocky, his soaked clothing clung to his chilled body, his arm throbbed, and there was a relentless pounding in his skull.

He shivered, then groaned as a thousand other aches and pains vibrated to agonizing life. He stayed still for a moment, feeling as if he was on the losing end of a championship prizefight.

Or a landslide.

He sat up abruptly, making his tortured body scream in protest.

Brandon. Where was his partner?

Caleb dragged himself to his feet. Brilliant flashes of lightning illuminated the area. The tons of rock and mud that had detached themselves from the hillside had come to rest just yards away. He'd been lucky to escape. Had his partner?

"Brandon!"

Thunder drowned out his yell. When the rumble died away, he tried again. Picking his way over the shifting pile of rubble, he tried to figure out where his partner had been standing when all hell had broken loose.

At a stream of rushing water, Caleb remembered. Brandon had been on the opposite side. Using a tree branch to keep himself steady, he started across the now knee-deep rapids. Branches and stones pummeled his legs, mud sucked at his boots. Bruised and breathless, he pulled himself onto the bank. He allowed himself only a few moments to rest and fill his lungs.

"Brandon!"

Desperate to find his partner, he dug in the mud with his bare hands. He shoved aside branches and kicked at rocks, calling out Brandon's name until he was hoarse. Still he found no sign of his partner, or Jim Driscoe.

A shaft of hatred went through him at the thought of the drug dealer, who had put them in this situation.

Suddenly he heard a buzzing in his ears and the night got darker. "Dammit! I am not going to pass out."

Disoriented and dizzy, he leaned against a tree. Letting the bulky trunk take his weight, Caleb wiped the moisture from his eyes. When lightning flashed again, he stared at his fingers. They were wet with not water, but blood. He closed his eyes, the smell of wet earth and leaves filling his nostrils.

Fatigue overtook him. Suddenly the ground didn't look so hard and rocky. Would it hurt if he just lay down and slept for a while?

His foggy mind recognized the signs of concussion, and he shook away the thought. Forget sleep, he ordered himself. He pushed away from the tree that had been holding him up and lost his footing on the slick ground. Reaching out, his left hand made contact with a branch, which he used to lever himself up.

Swaying on rubbery legs, Caleb had to admit he wasn't going to be able to find his partner on his own. Sliding around in the mud was getting him nowhere. He had to have help.

Lightning flashed, blinding him temporarily, and the boom of thunder that followed reverberated in his head. The pain drove him to his knees. *Get up, Caleb, get up!* he ordered. On legs of oatmeal, he staggered to his feet.

And walked.

With a hammer using his brain for an anvil and his

arm still throbbing, Caleb concentrated on putting one foot in front of the other. Right. Left. Right. Left.

Rain saturated his clothing, weighing him down. After a while he didn't even try to stop the shivering that racked his body.

Lightning and thunder dogged him every step of the way.

Right. Left. Right. Left.

The words became a litany.

His feet were cold, so cold. His toes squished numbly inside his boots, whatever water repellent they'd once had no match for the sopping terrain.

He had to stop. He had to sit. Only the thought of Brandon, unconscious and alone, kept him moving.

And then he saw it.

A light. Faint. Flickering.

Keeping his gaze focused on that dim welcoming glow, Caleb forced his tired body on. The forest floor was uneven, covered with dead leaves and needles. Wet ferns and vines grabbed at his knees. At one point he stumbled over a fallen log, wrenching his ankle and falling hard on his injured arm. He hissed in a sharp breath, then lay for a moment on the ground, his lungs aching. Angry for his weakness, he pushed up.

Pain bit at his arm, but he welcomed it. As long as the pain stood by him, he wouldn't be able to surrender to the lethargy the concussion caused.

He limped toward the light. His head pounded as thunder reverberated through the night. But he kept moving. He was not going to let those drug-dealing dogs get the best of him.

After what seemed like an eternity, Caleb finally arrived at the cabin. He made his way around the Jeep parked out front. Not sure what he would find, he reached around to the small of his back for his gun.

It wasn't there.

He checked the pockets of his soaked denim jacket. Nothing. *Great, just great,* he berated himself. *You've lost your only weapon.*

In the dim light from a window, he saw the outline of a woodpile on the porch. He eased up the steps and picked up a log, a piece of branch really, just thick enough to get someone's attention if necessary. Then he made his way to the window and peered inside.

The interior seemed warm and welcoming. A rectangular chopping-block table divided the living room from the kitchen. The furniture was old-fashioned and comfortable-looking. Oil lamps provided light, along with the flames from a huge stone fireplace.

Then he saw a woman standing in front of the stove, stirring something in a saucepan.

Caleb couldn't smell the food, but his stomach growled, anyway. He hadn't eaten since he and Brandon had stopped for doughnuts and coffee before heading up to the mountains.

Thinking about his friend and partner reminded him of his priorities. Food and bed could wait. He needed a phone.

For a few minutes he stayed at the window, but seeing no other signs of life, he turned to make his way to the front door.

The movement sent stars shooting through his head so violently that he fell to one knee. The branch dropped from his nerveless fingers and clattered to the porch. Afraid he'd black out, he stayed still for a couple of moments, drawing in deep breaths, then cautiously rose.

But the buzzing in his ears wouldn't go away, and the night started to close in on him. Caleb hung on to the railing, fighting the faint. One step at a time, he followed the porch to the front door, the hold on his consciousness beginning to slip.

As he raised his fist to knock on the door, he cracked his right arm against the jamb. The pain that shot through him was more than he could bear. Almost instantly he collapsed.

Chapter Two

A flash of lightning illuminated Shannon Garrett's shadowy kitchen, followed quickly by the boom of thunder. Turning from the stove where she stirred the soup that was to be her dinner, she glanced through the window over the sink. Rain battered the diamond-shaped panes, blotting out her view. The wind outside howled like a wounded animal.

A strange prickly feeling came over her. This was going to be one hell of a storm, she thought. Thank heavens for propane tanks and oil lamps. It might be days before her electricity came back on.

She swung back to the stove and turned off the burner. The delicious smell of her homemade chicken soup wafted through the cabin, but she'd lost interest in eating. Suddenly, being alone, miles from civilization, didn't seem like such a good idea. The storm and the dark were eerie. Shadows lurked in the corners of her small log cabin, making it feel claustrophobic, no longer the refuge it had been the past three years.

"Don't be ridiculous, Shannon."

The sound of her voice made her feel a little better. She was being silly. More for something to do than out of hunger, she took an oversize mug from the cupboard next to the sink and began to ladle soup into it.

A loud thump outside startled her. She paused to listen. A tree branch falling? When no other sound penetrated the howl of the storm, she went back to her soup.

Another loud bump made her heart rise to her throat. She stood absolutely still, head cocked, listening to the too-human sound of the wind groaning in the trees. Lightning illuminated the room like a strobe while thunder drowned out all other sounds. The silence that followed was broken by another skin-tingling groan. The door rattled as if something heavy had fallen against it.

Shannon put down the ladle, then opened a drawer and took out two large flashlights. Listening intently, she walked slowly to the front door. She wished it had a peephole. But then, without a porch light, she wouldn't be able to see who it was anyway.

A flashlight in each hand, Shannon forced herself to be logical. It wasn't likely that anyone was out there. The cabin was miles from her closest neighbor, even more miles from the main road. The few people who knew where she lived didn't casually drop in on her. The noises that had spooked her were probably just those of a raccoon seeking shelter from the storm.

Still, she had to be smart here. This part of the Santa Cruz Mountains was remote enough to hide all kinds of criminal activity. It would be naive to ignore the facts. She turned on one of the flashlights.

Another crash against the door made her jump.

"Who is it?" Her voice sounded pathetically shaky.

"Open the door...need to..."

It was a man's voice, and Shannon moved closer to the door. "Who's out there? What do you want?"

Silence.

She held her breath. It was stupid to assume the man who'd answered her call had just gone away. The voice had been barely audible, but the plea had been clear. She'd have to be made of stone to ignore it.

Holding one flashlight over her head like a club, Shannon eased the door open slowly. She shone the other light on what looked like a large pile of wet rags on her front porch. The clump of fabric moved, the weak beam of the flashlight revealing a dark-haired man who lay on his side. His face was pale, his brows drawn together. His jaw was tight, as if he was gritting his teeth.

Keeping the light on him, Shannon moved onto the porch. "Are you all right? What happened to you?"

From the looks of him the man was far from all right. It was perhaps a silly question under the circumstances, but then, Shannon had never been in this situation before.

Using his left hand, he pushed himself to a sitting position. "Landslide," he said, his voice as deep and dark as the night. He looked up at her with eyes the color of blue ice. Under several days' growth of beard, his face was hard and drawn with pain. "Won't hurt you...promise."

Making what she suspected was a very foolish decision, Shannon set both flashlights on a table just inside the door, then reached down to help him up. He flinched when she touched his upper right arm.

Wondering if the flinch was involuntary or just a means of stalling, Shannon looked around cautiously.

Was someone else out there? When lightning lit up the area around the cabin, all she saw were trees and her Jeep. No other vehicles.

"Are you alone?" Would he tell her if he wasn't? Shannon thought dryly.

"Yeah."

"How did you get here?"

He rose to one knee, bracing his hand on the wall for support. "Walked."

"That must have been some walk."

A gust of wind blew rain onto the porch, dampening her sweater and jeans. She really had no choice—she couldn't leave the man out in the rain. Crouching on his left, she used both hands to help him stand. "Let's get you inside before we both drown. We can discuss the hows and whys later."

Her visitor leaned heavily on her as she guided him into the cabin. He was big, his body hard and muscular. His clothes were soaked through, and he was shivering. She led him to the couch. "Here, sit down in front of the fire."

He slumped onto the couch. His eyes met hers for a second, then rolled back in his head as he passed out.

Shannon stared at her unconscious guest. Big and dark, he had a compelling face. Not exactly handsome, yet the kind of face that drew a woman's attention, making her wonder if he was a saint or a sinner.

A cut at his hairline oozed blood, but a huge lump on his forehead drew her attention. Not wanting to hurt him, she touched it gingerly. No wonder he'd passed out. He probably had a concussion. Standing back, she saw that the rest of his body wasn't in much better shape than his head.

His face and hands had several bruises and scratches. His black denim jeans were muddy and torn at the knees, as if he'd fallen. His jacket had a tear on the right arm. In short, he looked as if he'd gone through quite an ordeal.

Working as quickly and quietly as possible in the dim light, Shannon gathered the items she figured she'd need. With the help of one of the flashlights, she found the first-aid kit in the cupboard under the bathroom sink. She brought the kit, towels and a washcloth back to the living room and set them on the coffee table. In the kitchen she filled the teapot with bottled water, placed it on the burner and turned on the flame. It heated quickly. Deciding she'd need more light, she took the kitchen lantern and set it next to the one on the coffee table.

She returned to the kitchen and poured the warmed water in a mixing bowl. When she picked up the bowl, the water sloshed over the side. With shaking hands, she set it down and took a deep breath.

Relax, Shannon, she ordered herself. *He's just a human being who needs your help. Nothing more, nothing less. He can't hurt you in his condition.*

The pep talk didn't work. Not when she knew better. Some people had no qualms about hurting others. Even people who claimed to love you hurt you. It would be unwise to assume this man meant no harm just because he'd been injured. His incapacity was only temporary.

Hugging herself in an effort to steady her nerves, Shannon walked over to the couch and looked down at him. She tried to read who he was by his appearance, for it was all she had to go on right now. His dark hair, still glossy from the rain, fell over his broad forehead, reminding her of a little boy who refused to comb his hair. But one glance at his hard face told her he was no boy. He was a man, a stranger.

Who knew where he'd come from? Could he be one of the drug dealers who were rumored to live in the hills?

She had to laugh at herself. The man could just as easily be one of the many computer programmers who commuted over the hill to Silicon Valley every day. Or he could be one of the retro hippies who thought Santa Cruz was the land of peace and love. Yet she'd automatically assumed he was a criminal on the run. She'd been buried in the hills so long her imagination was having a field day.

Of course, that still didn't explain what this man had been doing wandering around in a storm so far from civilization.

He moved, emitting a low moan as some ache made itself known. Shannon responded to his pain. What did it matter who he was? He was hurt. He needed care. Until the power and phones were restored, she was his only chance of survival. So until then, she would just have to do what had to be done.

Her resolve set, she went back to the kitchen to retrieve the bowl of warm water. His wounds would need to be cleaned. She checked to make sure she had everything, then knelt in front of the couch.

She saw him shiver and knew his clothes would have to come off. Because of the way he'd reacted when she'd touched his arm, she decided to start from the bottom and work up. If he had a concussion, she knew she'd have to wake him soon, but she preferred he stay unconscious for the better part of her ministrations.

With hands held steady by determination, Shannon untied his shoes. She tugged off his muddy boots and set them aside. The dirty wet socks stuck stubbornly to his icy skin, but eventually gave in. She dunked a washcloth in the warm water and washed the dirt off his feet. His toes were long, the nails neatly trimmed. The sight of them eased some of her fears. She couldn't imagine a drug dealer or murderer taking such care with his personal hygiene.

She gazed at the man dripping rainwater and mud on her sofa and wondered what act of recklessness had sent him out in a storm. An anger that felt way too familiar rose inside her. Sometimes she wondered if there was a man in the world who had the common sense to use the brains God gave him. They all thought they were invincible.

"And it's left to us women to pick up the pieces."

No response came from the unconscious stranger.

She leaned over to undo his belt. The jeans had to come off. Shannon pulled and tugged at them, but the muddy material clung to the man's muscular thighs. She fought with the stubborn denim, struggling inch by inch to push it down his legs. "Come on, big guy, help me out here."

Finally victorious, she tossed the jeans aside, then turned back. The sight of his white briefs made nearly transparent from the damp, had her drawing a sharp breath.

She'd been with one man in her life. She'd only *seen* one man naked in her life. She averted her gaze, feeling as if she'd invaded the man's privacy.

He shivered violently, and Shannon realized her

shyness was not only immature, but possibly dangerous to the man's health. What did privacy matter to
a person who was injured and cold?

Feeling a little unnerved anyway, she stripped off
the briefs. She kept her gaze on his face as she draped
a bath towel over his hips.

Glad to have the task completed, Shannon took a
few minutes to wash the dirt and blood off his long
muscular legs. She treated and bandaged the cuts on
his knees, wishing there was something she could do
to ease the painful-looking bruises, too. The more she
saw of him, the more she realized what an ordeal he
must have been through.

She moved up to sit beside him. She didn't want
to hurt him, but she had to see how his arm was under
the jacket. She started on his left side, moving the
sleeve down his arm slowly. In spite of her care, he
moaned. He pushed weakly at her, trying to fight her
off.

"Don't! Leave me alone!" His eyes remained
closed. He seemed to be in the middle of a nightmare.
"Have to find Brandon. Have to find Brandon."

"I don't know who Brandon is, big guy, but you're
not going anywhere."

His eyes opened suddenly, pale blue and feverish
in his dark face. "Who are you?"

She smiled, relieved he was awake. "Shannon.
How about you?"

He eyed her suspiciously. "What am I doing
here?" He sat up gingerly. "Where are my pants?"
He tried to stand, causing the towel to drop to the
floor, leaving him bare from the waist down. He
swayed and dropped back onto the couch, clutching

his head with his good arm. "God, my head hurts like hell."

Cheeks flushed, Shannon replaced the towel, then took an instant-ice pack out of the first-aid kit and handed it to him. "Here, hold this on that bump. It looks like you took quite a knock. It's possible you have a concussion."

The man did as he was told, evidently realizing he wasn't in any shape to argue. "There was a landslide. The last thing I remember was a rock or something hitting me in the head." He took the ice off his head and looked at her. "How'd I get here?"

Shannon reached over and guided the hand with the pack back to his head. "Keep that there." His big hand was warm, but not feverish. Feeling a little tingle from the contact, she drew her fingers from his. "I have no idea how you got here. I found you collapsed on my porch not long after the electricity went out."

He nodded, winced, then laid his head against the back of the sofa and closed his eyes.

Shannon could see he was hurting, but she didn't want him falling asleep again. She knew the first twenty-four hours in a concussion were crucial. She had to keep him talking. What's more, she had to find out who he was. "What's your name?"

"My name?" His voice slurred. "What's my name?"

He sounded as if he was about to doze off. "You said something about a landslide?" she asked.

She heard the trace of suspicion in her own voice. Caleb opened his eyes, and she realized he'd heard it, too. "The ground started to shake," he told her. "I looked up and it seemed like the whole mountain was coming down on me. I tried to run for cover. The next thing I knew, I was hit and everything went black.''

"Do you know how long you were out?"

He looked at his watch, and she saw that the crystal was cracked. The time had stopped at three o'clock.

"What time is it now?" he asked.

"About seven." Four hours, she thought, a long time to be wandering around in a storm. "Do you know how far you walked?"

Caleb tried to come up with an answer to her question, but cold seemed to seep through to his bones, making him shiver. He dropped the ice pack and wrapped his arms around his chest, but the dampness of his shirt and jacket only made his trembling worse.

Shannon placed the ice pack on the coffee table. "We'll figure it out later. We've got to get the rest of your wet clothes off."

Caleb looked at her. She was a beautiful woman. Tall, with feminine curves, tawny-gold hair and skin like satin. Her eyes were shadowed, full of secrets, the color indistinguishable in the flickering light. He'd certainly never expected to find an angel in the midst of hell, but it appeared that was exactly what he'd done. If circumstances had been different, he would have enjoyed hanging around for a while.

But his partner was out there in the storm. A vicious drug dealer was after them both. He couldn't forgive himself if he led trouble here, to the home of an innocent woman.

If she was innocent... He gathered the towel around his hips and rose slowly. How did he know he could trust her? What if the Driscoes and Larkin showed up? Would she just turn him over? His head throbbed in time with his heartbeat. Just because she'd taken in a stray didn't mean she wouldn't cave in to pressure, endangering both him and his partner. He had to get out of here. "Do you have a phone I can use?"

Shannon stood beside him. "Phone lines are down, along with the power."

Caleb's head started to swim. "You don't understand. I have to make a call."

"I'm sorry. That's not possible right now."

He tried to listen to what she was saying, but he couldn't make sense of the words. He swayed, then felt strong arms go around him.

"Hang on, big guy."

Her voice was gentle, kind, with a touch of humor. He did what she said and hung on. And found a gentleness he'd never known. He wanted to sink into the softness, to savor it.

Her arms tightened. "Don't pass out yet," she commanded sternly. "We have to get you to the bed."

Caleb's woozy mind thought bed sounded like a great idea. He imagined cool sheets and a tawny-haired woman lying beside him as he explored her luscious curves. He felt a stirring in his loins, then realized he'd dropped his covering. "The towel."

"Don't worry about it," she said matter-of-factly, guiding him along. "You'll be under the blankets in no time."

They entered a dimly lit room.

"Come on, just a few more feet."

A few more feet. It felt like a mile.

"Okay, sit."

She pushed him back gently until he felt a mattress

give beneath him. The quilts had been drawn back, and the sheets felt cool against his skin. He started to shiver again. He grabbed at the blankets and tried to lie down.

Shannon held him up. "Oh, no, you don't. We need to get your jacket off and your shirt, too."

She tugged at his jacket. At her urging, he moved his arm out of the sleeve. She slid off the right sleeve, sending fire through his arm. He gasped involuntarily.

"Sorry. I'll take care of that as soon as we take off the shirt."

Caleb tried to tell her he understood, but when he looked at her bending over him, her lovely face intent, her hair spilling around her shoulders like golden silk, he couldn't form the words.

He reached out to touch a skein of her hair. It felt like the finest silk. "God, you're beautiful." His voice sounded as though it came from the other end of a tunnel.

She frowned a little. "We really have to take care of that arm. So help me take off this shirt of yours, okay?"

He suddenly felt very tired. "Okay, then can I go to sleep?"

"For a little while," she said in a serious voice.

With her help, he took off his long-sleeved knit shirt. Then he lay on his left side, his head against the cool pillows. He felt her draw a blanket over him.

"I'm going to get the first-aid kit."

Caleb closed his eyes against the pounding in his head. "I'll wait here, all right?"

"All right, big guy."

He liked the way she said "big guy" and wondered if hearing her say his name would sound as sweet.

"Caleb," he said as a black hole started to swallow him. "My name is Caleb."

"All right, Caleb."

A half smile revealed a dimple in his right cheek. Shannon watched him sleep for a few minutes. Maybe he wasn't as hard as he looked.

Or felt.

But the last thought was quickly quashed. She turned and left the room. A sensible woman didn't think such thoughts about an injured stranger who landed on her doorstep. Even if the stranger was lying naked in her bed.

Especially because he was lying naked in her bed.

If being with Tony had taught her nothing else, it had taught her that she was better off being sensible. The roller coaster of their life together had left her at the bottom, hurt and disoriented. She had no intention of getting on that ride again. Its effects were devastating.

Retrieving the first-aid kit from the living room, Shannon returned to find Caleb dozing against the pillows. The quilt had fallen down around his waist, revealing his bare chest. Shannon's breath caught. Broad, tanned, with a black mat of hair, his chest revealed that he was indeed a big strong man. A spurt of longing went through her, in spite of her earlier resolve to be sensible. He looked solid, down-to-earth, the kind of man who would walk through hell to protect a woman, the kind to hold that woman forever.

She turned away abruptly. She had no right to be looking at the man as anything other than someone hurt and in need. Just because she hadn't had much human contact since she'd lost Tony didn't mean she should turn this man into a romantic fantasy, even if he was tall, dark, dangerously attractive and mysterious as the night.

Shannon walked back to the foot of the bed. *He's a stranger,* she reminded herself deliberately. Once the storm was over, he would go back to his own life, leaving her to her solitude. That was the way she wanted it, and that was how it would be.

Caleb opened his eyes and smiled wryly. "I can't seem to stay awake."

Hardening her heart against his vulnerability, Shannon moved around the bed to his right side and set the first-aid kit down on the quilt. "You've been through quite an ordeal," she said stiffly. "It's only natural your body should want to rest and recover." *God,* she thought, *I sound like some frightened schoolmarm.* The man could barely stay awake. What did she think he was going to do to her?

Caleb's eyelids drifted shut again.

Shannon frowned, worried a little about his sleepiness. She'd done enough research on the subject of concussion to know she mustn't let him sleep long.

His eyes opened suddenly. "What ordeal?"

Shannon raised a brow. His question had bordered on suspicious, which seemed a strange reaction. "You mentioned a landslide. Don't you remember it?"

He gazed at her for a moment as if trying to read her mind. "It all happened so fast."

His answer unsettled her a little. It sounded like the truth, yet she sensed something more was going on. She thought about questioning him, then decided against it. The man had been banged around so much he probably didn't have any idea what he was saying. Besides, it didn't really matter to her, anyway.

She turned her attention to his arm. "I'm going to clean this and put some antibiotic ointment on it. I'll try not to hurt you."

Caleb nodded. "Do what you have to. I really appreciate everything you've done. A woman alone, you could have left me out on the doorstep."

"Well, it did cross my mind," she admitted, venturing a smile.

She looked at the deep red groove on his upper arm. Suddenly she didn't feel like smiling.

What had she done? What kind of man had she taken into her home? Only one thing could have made a wound like that.

A bullet.

She stepped back from the bed. "Who are you?"

His light-blue eyes showed bewilderment. "What's wrong?"

Shannon glared at him. "You didn't receive that cut in any landslide. That wound came from a gun. Someone shot at you and grazed your arm. Now, I want to know who you are and what you're doing in these hills."

Chapter Three

The fact that Shannon was more angry than afraid intrigued Caleb. A woman alone in a remote cabin, a wounded stranger collapses on her doorstep. Turns out he's been shot. It would be only natural for her to feel fear at her discovery. But the angry flush on Shannon's cheeks showed nothing of the kind. He wondered why.

Hands on hips, Shannon glared at him. "I'd like an answer, Caleb, or whatever your name is."

She was really something. It took guts to question a stranger when there was a very real possibility he could be dangerous. Because of that, his first instinct was to reassure her. His second told him that reassuring her couldn't be his first priority. She might be gutsy and gorgeous, but she was still an unknown quantity.

"Well?" she said impatiently.

Time for some fast thinking. He'd already made the mistake of giving her his first name, but that didn't mean he had to tell her the last, or his reason for showing up on her doorstep bloody and torn, beyond the landslide.

He'd learned in his undercover work that the key

to successfully hiding your identity was to keep as close to the truth as possible. "My name is Caleb Joseph," he said, using his middle name. "A friend and I were visiting a cabin up here."

"In the middle of one of the worst winters this area has known?"

He shrugged off her suspicion. "We didn't know the hillside was going to fall down on us."

"I can imagine," she said dryly. "So what were you doing up here?" She glanced at his arm. "Hunting?"

The horror that filled her gaze brought an immediately denial. "Of course not!"

He realized his mistake just as her eyes narrowed.

"Dammit, I should have known. You're a cop, aren't you?" The conclusion seemed to raise her ire even more.

He regarded her with genuine surprise. "What makes you say that?"

"The lack of detailed information in your answer. And the fact that you have a bullet wound, yet you weren't hunting. Either you're a cop or you're a criminal."

Good deduction, he thought. Convincing his hostess that she had nothing to fear without revealing his identity was going to be harder than he thought. "Well, I hate to disappoint you, but the gunshot wound was the result of a ricochet, just some guys doing target practice." He thought it better not to mention that he was the target. "And I work in computers." Everything he'd said was the truth, as far as it went.

She still looked skeptical. Time to try a different tack. "I have to say I'm a little surprised by your earlier reaction. Most people would be thrilled to find out they had a cop collapse on their doorstep, rather than some criminal on the run.''

''I'm not most people,'' she snapped. ''One was enough.'' She crossed her arms in front of her chest. ''And *you* are not some dweeb from Silicon Valley, so cut the bull.''

''A man can work in the computer industry and not be a dweeb,'' he countered, doing his best to sound offended.

He didn't know what to make of the bitterness that edged her voice, and his head ached from trying. He closed his eyes and reached up his good hand to try to rub away the pain. The logical answer was that she'd had a run-in with the cops. Which put her on the other side of the law. But Caleb couldn't see this beautiful caring woman as a criminal. Petty or otherwise. Damn, he wished he didn't have such a headache. It made it hard to think clearly.

He opened his eyes. ''How did you know a bullet made the mark on my arm?''

''Personal experience,'' she said stiffly.

''Really?'' Disbelief colored his voice. His instincts told him she was as innocent as she looked. ''Were you the grazer or the grazee?''

''Neither.''

This time Caleb recognized a hint of pain behind the anger. Whoever had been injured was someone she'd cared about. Her father? Brother? Husband?

''Then who?''

''I don't want to talk about it.'' She moved to the bed and picked up a sterile pad. ''We need to finish this.'' She started swabbing at his wound.

The antiseptic stung, and he flinched.

"Sorry." She continued more gently.

Once it was clean, she slathered on the ointment, then covered the wound with a new piece of gauze, fixing it to his arm with white tape. Her hands were gentle and competent as she wound the bandage around his arm. Her silky hair brushed his bare shoulder. She smelled of rain and wood smoke. Scents he would never have considered erotic until now.

Knowing his turn of thought was completely inappropriate, he stared straight ahead and tried to concentrate on the natural weaving that hung on the opposite wall. It was fashioned of driftwood and pinecones and thick earth-toned yarn. He liked it. But even as he studied the unusual work of art, he couldn't ignore the fact that if he turned his head another inch, he could taste Shannon's full wide mouth.

He felt his body warm at the thought and knew he should do something, anything, to dampen the burgeoning spark. Women like Shannon had a way of complicating things. They made a man want to solve every problem, explore every secret. And then they left you wanting. He didn't need that kind of complication. His best bet was to stay as far away from her as possible.

Seconds later Shannon finished her task. Without saying a word she picked up the first-aid kit and turned to leave the room.

"Shannon?"

She stopped and looked over her shoulder. "Yes?"

"You don't have to worry." He smiled. "I really am harmless."

She gazed at him for several seconds. "A harmless computer guy who just happened to be visiting in the area,'' she said sweetly, ''and just happened to get himself shot and just happened to get caught in a landslide?''

He had to admit the woman would have made a great interrogator. A less-experienced cop might have been ready to confess here and now. And so would he. Later. When he was sure she was out of harm's way.

For now he just smiled wryly. ''What can I say? I'm a klutz.''

Her own smile was grim. ''Well, try not to fall out of bed, all right?'' Then she left the room.

Against his will Caleb waited for her to come back. Impatient with himself, impatient for her presence, he found himself a victim of the very complication he'd dreaded.

He wanted to talk to her. He wanted to know why she was so bitter. He wanted to soothe away the hurt. He wasn't the only one with something to hide. There were secrets behind her anger and pain. What man had hurt her so badly?

He caught himself again, pulled himself back. *She doesn't need or want you, buddy. So put away the sword and shield. The woman might be a damsel in distress, but she's obviously determined to fight her own battles. And you have your own problems.*

Brandon. His partner and best friend could even now be lying under tons of rock and mud. Had he escaped, only to run smack into Jim Driscoe? Or even worse, that weasel Larkin? Caleb shifted on the bed. His body screamed in protest.

He lay still until the din eased. Once he was able to relax a little, he had to laugh at himself. Who was he to be thinking about slaying dragons?

Hell, his own dragon had nearly devoured him. A months-long undercover investigation had blown up in his face. A landslide had come close to burying him forever. He had a concussion that kept his head banging constantly, and he was stuck in the middle of nowhere while his partner was out there alone. He had enough to worry about without dragging out the armor and steed to go jousting with the demons of a woman who'd just as soon toss him out in the rain.

SHANNON PUT AWAY the first-aid supplies and tried not to think about the man who lay on her bed. No stranger had ever affected her so thoroughly. Her fingers still tingled from touching the firm strength of his arms. Those weren't the muscles of a man who spent his life in a high-tech firm.

She saw the soup waiting for her, but her appetite had fled. She poured the cooled soup back into the pot and put the mug in the sink, along with a few dishes from earlier. Washing them would give her something to do. She turned on the faucet, but no water came out. *Duh, Shannon,* she thought. *No power, no pump.*

She looked over at the computer that had been her lifeline. If she had electricity, she could work. As a syndicated advice columnist, she always had work to be done, letters to be answered, subjects that needed researching. Dealing with the problems of the faceless readers who wrote to her for advice was much easier than dealing with her own.

She rubbed her arms, feeling out of sorts. Having a man in the house was not doing her nerves any good. Especially when she suspected he was lying about his identity. Which made her physical reaction to him all the more frustrating. She wished she could take a long walk to work off her restlessness, but the deluge outside would likely drown her.

Letting out a long sigh, she opened the old trunk where she kept extra blankets and took out a pile. She covered the couch, still damp and dirty thanks to her unexpected guest. Sitting, she stared at the fire in the hearth and wished with all her might that the storm would end, the power would come on, the phones would work, and her guest would go home.

But even as she wished, she knew it was futile. She'd seen storms like this before. By now the stream at the foot of her property would have flooded the road. Even if she could get safely through it with her four-wheel-drive, that didn't guarantee passage on other area roads. Caleb's landslide probably wouldn't be the only one.

The thought of spending several days with this handsome stranger, who suddenly didn't feel like such a stranger, unnerved her. She hadn't lived with another person for three years, and she'd come to like it that way. No disagreements, no fights, no dispute over what to have for dinner, what to watch on TV, when to get a new car.

No love, a little voice added.

What did love have to do with it? she scoffed. Love was useless. Love promised everything, but in the end it left you with nothing. She didn't need love anymore. She needed her work and she needed her solitude. And thanks to this storm, she had neither.

She crossed to the fireplace and added a couple of logs. What she had was a perfectly normal female reaction to a big handsome male. Hormones. If he wasn't here, she'd be sitting by the fire, wrapped in an afghan, enjoying the sound of the rain.

Alone.

The last time she'd visited Santa Cruz, she'd bought several books she looked forward to reading. What better time to do that than when you were stuck inside on a rainy night?

Alone.

Shannon closed the screen and went back to the couch. In spite of the glowing heat, she felt chilled. She grabbed the afghan off the back of the sofa and draped it over her shoulders. Still she shivered. Damn him for showing up on her doorstep and disrupting her quiet peaceful evening.

She did not want him here. She didn't need the warmth that radiated from him. She didn't need his problems.

She didn't care how many times he told her he worked in computers. She had a hard time believing it. But she couldn't come up with a reason he'd lie about his identity, either.

Well, liar or not, she didn't want the responsibility of taking care of him. Tending his wounds had brought back her experience with Tony as vividly as if it were yesterday. She did not want to patch up another man just to have him turn around and get shot again. She'd barely survived the first time.

"Shannon?"

She jerked around and saw Caleb leaning against the back of the couch. He'd wrapped the quilt around himself, and his face was pale from exertion.

All thoughts of the past faded. She jumped up and went to him. "For heaven's sake, what are you—

Never mind. Come and sit down before you fall down.''

She put her arm around his wide back and guided him to the couch. It seemed incongruous that she should be helping a man who made her feel tiny and vulnerable. Yet when she looked at his mouth, pinched with pain he'd probably scoff at, she couldn't help feeling protective.

As he sat on the couch, the quilt slipped from around his shoulders, reminding her that he wore nothing underneath. Not that she'd really forgotten. That would have been as hard as ignoring the fact that he was a man. A dangerously attractive man, with a dimple charming enough to make the hardest woman melt at his feet.

''You must be cold,'' she said, hoping he'd take the hint and cover himself.

He looked up at her. ''I'm fine.''

His blue gaze met hers. His eyes were quite beautiful, she thought involuntarily. Clear and shiny, like the sky reflected in a raindrop. They seemed to see inside her, sense things Shannon didn't want to share.

She looked away. He was much too compelling. She'd told herself her reaction had nothing to do with him, but that wasn't exactly the truth. Taking him into her home, she'd probably saved his life. It didn't matter that he was a stranger, and a lying one at that. She still didn't want to pick up the newspaper next week or next month and see an article reporting the death of Caleb Joseph in some freak accident. Thinking of those beautiful blue eyes cold and lifeless hurt her heart in a way she hadn't felt since she'd lost Tony.

Not liking the path her mind had taken, Shannon searched for an out and found it. ''I put some chicken soup on the stove earlier. I'm sure it's been hours since you've eaten."

Caleb shook his head. "Thanks, but I'm not really hungry. If you'll give me my clothes, I'll get out of your hair."

She raised an eyebrow at him. The concussion had obviously scrambled his brain. "I'm afraid you're going to have to accept my hospitality for a while longer." She walked over to the stove and turned on the burner.

"Shannon, it's not that I don't appreciate your taking me in and taking care of me, but I have to check on my friend. He got caught in the landslide, too. I really need to borrow your Jeep."

"It won't do any good," Shannon told him patiently as she stirred the soup. He really sounded worried. Her heart went out to him.

And that has to stop right now, she ordered herself. *You're better off treating him like one of your readers. A stranger looking for expert advice.* Though she'd never felt less like an expert.

"It's a four-wheel drive," he persisted. "Surely it'll be able to negotiate a little flooding."

Lightning flashed, followed immediately by thunder so loud it rattled the windows. Shannon turned on him, hands on hips. "Are you paying attention at all? The Santa Cruz Mountains don't know what 'a little flooding' means. It's been raining off and on for weeks. Power lines are down. The hills are saturated. The landslide that almost buried you wasn't the first this winter and it won't be the last. Until the rain stops, you're just going to have to stay put."

She swung back to the stove. This was really something, having to convince the man to stay when she didn't want him here in the first place!

The soup started to simmer. She picked up the wooden spoon and stirred it. "Besides, your right arm is injured. How do you propose to drive a stick shift?" Realizing that might sound like a challenge, Shannon hurried on, "But if you're really set on leaving, I guess I could drive you."

"Absolutely not!"

Shannon turned to look at him. "I beg your pardon?"

"There's no way in hell I'd let you drive in this kind of weather. The roads are far too dangerous and—" Caleb stopped abruptly. "You did that on purpose, didn't you?"

Shannon shrugged and picked up a soup mug and ladle. Reverse psychology. Tony had used it on her so often that she'd picked up the trick herself. She filled the mug, then found a spoon and returned to the couch.

He looked up at her, eyes narrowed. She could almost hear the wheels turning. She held the mug out to him. "Go ahead. You won't lose any macho points by eating a little soup."

He took it. "This isn't macho posturing. There are people out there who are counting on me."

"Counting on you to what? Fix their computers?" she asked innocently. "Since there's no electricity for miles, I bet they can wait." She took her own mug and crossed to the rocking chair next to the fireplace. "Besides, you're not going to be much help to those people if you're dead. Driving around in the rain with a concussion is not conducive to good health." An understatement to be sure, and the reason she refused to tell him about Tony's automatic four-wheel-drive pickup truck sitting in her garage. He might be capable of driving it, but that didn't guarantee he wouldn't end up in a ditch. "When the weather calms down a little, I'll drive you wherever you want to go. For now you're stuck, so you might as well enjoy your soup."

Obediently Caleb ate a spoonful. He couldn't argue with her logic, but it wasn't going to be easy waiting around until he could safely leave. Well, one thing he could be grateful for: If he couldn't get out, then no one could get in. Which meant he didn't have to worry about one of the Driscoes showing up looking for him.

He glanced over at Shannon. With the light behind her, her face was cast in shadows. He suspected she preferred it that way. Secrets and shadows.

"So who was the man who made you bury yourself in the wilds of the Santa Cruz Mountains?"

Shannon started at his deliberately abrupt question. "How do you know I'm not just staying here for a vacation?"

He glanced around the room, taking in the surroundings with a trained eye. "Bookshelves filled with books. Curtains on the windows. Furniture old but well cared for. Art on the walls. Way too homey to be only a temporary retreat. Besides, even the most dedicated techie doesn't travel around with all that state-of-the-art equipment." He gestured toward her computer. "I should know," he added. Even if she did suspect the lie, she couldn't be sure of the truth. It was safer that way. "So why don't you tell me about—"

"It's really none of your business," she said coolly.

And he might have let it go if he hadn't seen the flash of pain that crossed her face. "Well, the storm outside isn't letting up. And until it does, as you pointed out, you're stuck with me. We can't just sit and stare at each other."

"I'm sure we can come up with lots of subjects to discuss."

Yes, he thought, but none of them interested him as much as learning about the man who'd been idiotic enough to hurt this lovely woman. "He must have meant a lot to you."

She took a sip from her mug, then placed it carefully on the side table. "I really don't want to talk about this, Caleb, so—"

"You might not want to," he interrupted, "but you need to."

She wouldn't meet his eyes. "So now you're a psychologist?"

The sarcasm didn't bother him. It meant he'd gotten to her. He didn't know why this was so important, but it was. "You can be as rude as you like. It doesn't change the fact that you could use a sympathetic ear. And I need something to keep my mind off my friend."

Shannon searched his expression, looking for signs of manipulation. What she found was genuine concern. "Tony Garrett," she supplied, still a little reluctant. "He was my husband."

"Was?"

His expression was interested, not avidly curious. He wasn't looking for a sensational story. He was offering an ear.

Needing to move, she got to her feet and walked over to put her mug in the sink.

For days after Tony's death his fellow officers had dropped by. They'd offered her a shoulder to cry on, too. But she'd gotten the feeling that they needed to talk about Tony, to reassure themselves that the same thing wouldn't happen to them. When she'd tried to express her own frustration, they'd turned off. They didn't want to hear what their wives and girlfriends felt when their loved ones put their lives on the line time and time again.

She walked back into the living area. Caleb had set his empty mug on the coffee table. "Can I get you anything else?"

He shook his head. "Come sit down."

She sat on the opposite end of the couch from him. Two seat cushions separated them. It wasn't enough. She could feel the warmth radiating from him. His arms were tanned and muscular, their strength undiminished by the cuts and bruises that marred the flesh. Her fingers tingled as if remembering the texture of his skin.

She wrapped her arms around her waist to keep from reaching out. What the heck had gotten into her? Had she lived within her self-imposed seclusion so long that she was ready to throw herself at any man who came along?

"Shannon? Are you all right? I'm sorry I pressed you. If it's still too painful to talk about your husband..."

She looked at Caleb, saw the concern on his handsome face and knew that he was not just "any man."

"I'm fine." She clasped her hands in her lap. "I

was just thinking.'' About him, not about Tony, as Caleb must have thought.

The twinge of guilt that followed loosened her tongue. ''Tony was a police officer in San José. He was killed three years ago in the line of duty.''

''I'm sorry.''

The simple words eased the lump in her throat. Her friend Zoe had often told her she'd feel better if she talked about it, but she'd never been able to discuss Tony with anyone, even her best friend. Was that why she'd suddenly decided to talk? Or was it just a cover-up for her inappropriate feelings?

''Don't stop now.'' Caleb touched her hand.

The resulting tremor rocked her to her toes.

She pulled her hand back, looked away. Oh, no, she could not have this. He was a lost soul, just passing through. And she? She was even more lost than he was. No matter how her senses reacted to him, physical attraction did not equal a relationship. And even if it did, a relationship was the last thing she wanted.

''Shannon?'' he said softly. ''Tell me what happened.''

And because telling Tony's story suddenly seemed easier than dealing with her own feelings, she did.

''It wasn't the first time he'd been shot. Tony was very brave and capable. But his sense of responsibility for his fellow officers...'' She gazed into the fire, remembering. ''He was always first—the first to arrive, the first to volunteer.''

''The first to be wounded?''

She nodded. ''I can't count the times I had to go to the emergency room to pick him up.'' Gashes, knife wounds, bullets. ''Time after time, I'd tend

Tony's wounds. Time after time, he'd go back to the job." Eagerly, happily, as soon as he could, she remembered bitterly. "Being a police officer was his life."

"And in the end it was his death," Caleb said quietly.

Shannon nodded.

"I don't mean to be judgmental, but it sounds like he was reckless."

She half laughed, feeling no humor. "Men are. Haven't you noticed?"

Chapter Four

Caleb wanted to dispute it. He'd gotten his share of injuries, but he'd never rushed into the situations that had led to them. He'd gotten a reputation for knowing when to go and when to stay. It had saved his butt. It had saved his partners' butts. But after the way he'd landed on her doorstep, why should Shannon believe him?

Besides, now that he'd started the lie, he had to stay with it. For his, and her, own good.

He looked over at her. She sat staring into the fire. Light danced on her face and shot red highlights through her tawny hair. He still couldn't discern the color of her eyes, but he knew they didn't see the fire that set her smooth skin aglow. No, her eyes were focused on the past. On a man who had made police work his life.

He tried to understand Officer Tony Garrett. It should have been easy. Caleb had been a dedicated officer of the law since he'd graduated from the Police Academy at the age of twenty-two. Twelve years later he looked back on a decorated career he was proud of. But he hadn't had a loving wife waiting for him at home.

Shannon was a beautiful intelligent woman. Tony Garrett had been lucky to find her. How could the man keep putting himself in situations where in seconds he could lose everything?

Yet, knowing the kind of vicious criminals that plagued the world, Caleb thought a second later, how could he not? A real man, a real cop, couldn't go home to his family knowing he hadn't given his all to rid the streets of crime. It might be hard for the widow of a dead cop to understand, but...

Wanting very much to ease her pain, he reached out and touched her hand again.

She jumped as if she'd been burned, then got up to place another log on the fire.

"I hope you don't regret telling me about your husband," he said.

She shook her head and prodded the new log with the poker. "I moved here a couple of months after Tony died. Most of my communication is done over the computer or the telephone. I haven't talked to anyone about Tony in years."

Her delivery was so stoic that Caleb felt an urge to give her a shake. "I understand that becoming a widow at such a young age must have been hard on you, but don't you think three years is long enough to live as a recluse?"

She turned on him, poker still in hand. "You know nothing about me or why I choose to live the way I live, so keep your opinions to yourself."

Caleb immediately apologized. "You're right. Our acquaintance is too short for me to make such a judgment," he said formally. But he couldn't help thinking that he had hit a raw nerve. Was it possible the ice Shannon had encased herself in was thawing? It

seemed to him that her fiery reply could only mean
one thing. Shannon Garrett was returning to the land
of the living—and fighting it every step of the way.

She returned the poker to its rack. "If you don't
mind, I'd like to go to bed. I've been working since
six this morning. Since I'll be sleeping on the couch,
you'll have to go back to the bedroom."

The coldness of her request caused an equal and
opposite reaction in Caleb's lower regions. He looked
at Shannon, who stood stiffly, her head tossed back
as if ready for a fight.

"I know it's still fairly early," she added. "I hope
you don't mind."

Caleb bit back a laugh. The words may have been
polite, but the tone told him she didn't give a damn
whether he minded or not. How could a once-married
woman not realize what a challenge a haughty woman
presented to a man?

As much as he wanted to stay in the same room
with her, if she kept looking at him like a prickly
princess, with him in his weakened condition, he
didn't know if he could trust himself to keep from
kissing the frown off her face. He wrapped the quilt
around himself and stood. "It doesn't seem fair for
you to sleep on the damp couch."

"I'll be fine."

"Not sleeping on a damp couch," he insisted.
"Look, I could sleep on the floor. Or we could share
the bed."

The look she gave him could have felled a tree. "I
don't think so."

The line of her thought came through loud and
clear, irritating the hell out of him. "I'm not in any
shape to attack you."

"Go to bed, Caleb."

Since nothing he said seemed to convince her, he decided to give in gracefully. "Good night, Shannon, and thanks again."

He took a step. His bad ankle gave out on him and he lost his balance.

"Watch out!" Shannon exclaimed, moving to catch him.

His hand caught hers, and they both went down on the floor in a tangle. Though the patterned area rug cushioned the fall to some extent, pain rocketed through him.

"Caleb! Are you all right?"

Registering the concern in her voice, Caleb opened his eyes and looked straight into the most beautiful green eyes he'd ever seen. They reminded him of a forest at sunset, when the trees cast dark-green shadows and the sun dappled the forest floor with gold. He gazed into them, knowing if he looked long enough, he could uncover the secrets hidden in their mysterious depths.

"Caleb? Did you hurt yourself?" Shannon ran her hands along his bare torso, skimming over his chest and his ribs, as if looking for injury.

The touch of her hands on his body caused sensations he knew a man in his condition shouldn't be feeling. He took a deep breath, trying to slow the hot blood that raced through his veins.

It didn't work.

The quilt had been torn away when he fell, and the soft denim of her jeans rubbed against his lower body, causing an erotic friction that lit a fire in his loins. A man would have to be made of stone to ignore the luscious curves pressed against him, the warm breath mixing with his, the lush lips close enough to kiss.

"Would you please say something?" she prodded.

The exasperated plea got his attention. He smiled wryly. "You're going to have to get off me," he said, though he'd never wanted anything less in his life.

She flushed, then pushed herself up till she stood above him. Her eyes widened and she swung around so her back was to him. "I thought you were in shock," she accused.

He was, he thought. In shock because he wanted a woman—one he hadn't known even existed until a couple of hours ago—so much that he'd forgotten his injuries and his circumstances. He suspected Shannon Garrett could make him forget his own name.

"Caleb? Did you want some help up or should I just make you a bed on the floor?"

Caleb grabbed the quilt and wrapped it around his hips, wondering what she'd do if he took her up on her somewhat provocative offer. With regret he held out his hand. "You can turn around now."

She pulled him up but wouldn't quite look at him. "I think I can scare up some sweats that might fit you." She turned and walked to the bedroom.

He followed at a slower speed, favoring his left ankle. Entering the room, he found Shannon bent over, digging through the bottom drawer of a large oak dresser, presenting him with the sight of her denim-clad, nicely rounded backside. He groaned inwardly.

She stood up and turned to face him before he could hide his expression. She shot a glare at him that should have disintegrated him on the spot and tossed a pair of gray sweatpants and a sweatshirt onto the bed. ''Here, these should fit you.''

The worn but clean outfit boasted a San José State logo and certainly looked big enough for him. But he didn't really like the idea of dressing in another man's clothes. She'd already tarred him with the same brush as her reckless husband. The fact that she still had the clothes three years later surprised him.

He looked at her and saw she'd been studying him.

''Those aren't Tony's,'' she said quietly. ''They belonged to my father. He was a professor at San José State for thirty-five years. He and my mother retired to Northern California last year.''

He didn't know whether to be relieved or not by the information. On the one hand he was glad they hadn't belonged to her husband. But if they had, and she'd offered them, then it would have shown she was ready to move on with her life.

Whoa! Stop right there, he ordered himself. What difference did it make to him if a woman he hardly knew got over her dead husband? As soon as he could, he was out of here. He had to find Brandon and make sure the Driscoe operation was shut down.

''I'll let you get changed. Good night,'' Shannon said, turning to leave.

He caught her arm as she passed. ''Wait.''

Despite her thick sweater, Caleb felt the heat of her body and smelled the subtle fragrance of her skin. There was something about this woman that called to him. Something that made her achingly familiar, instead of the stranger she was.

A gust of wind sent rain clattering against the windows.

Shannon's gaze skittered away from his, focusing

on the dark square framing the black night. "Storm's picking up again."

She could say that again, he thought wryly. "Shannon."

Eyes shadowed by thick dark lashes gazed warily up at his face. "Is there something else you need?"

You. The answer was so definite in his mind it shocked him. How could that be, when he barely knew her? How could he need a stranger?

He looked at her face, so beautiful, so wary, so unwilling to trust. And who could blame her? He might not have the same reckless bent as her husband, but he did have a job to do. The Driscoe brothers had been showering cocaine on the local kids like it was snow. They were vicious dangerous criminals. And he wasn't going to stop until they were in prison.

"Caleb? Are you all right? Is your head hurting again?"

"A little," Caleb said, though the pounding seemed relentless. She'd done enough for him. "Nothing that a bit of sleep won't cure."

"I'll just get some things, then you can go to bed. But only for a while. If you do have a concussion—"

"Don't worry about it," he told her. He really had to get her out of there. "I've had concussions before. This was just a little knock on the head."

She didn't look convinced. She walked over to the closet and grabbed a nightgown and robe off a hook. Then she paused at the door. "Well, good night, then." Her voice was a little husky. She cleared her throat. "I put a jug of water in the bathroom, since the pump's not working right now. You'll find towels in the cabinet over the toilet and a new toothbrush in the one over the sink. Let me know if you need anything else.''

"Thanks," he told her. "Good night."

He waited until she left the room, then sat down on the bed, feeling every ache and pain…unable to deny that the biggest ache was for Shannon.

It was going to be a long night.

THE CLOCK CHIMED twelve times. Lying on the couch, Shannon counted every one. Just as she'd done at nine, ten and eleven. She twisted to lie on her side, facing the fireplace. Behind the screen, the flames licked at the log she'd added thirty minutes before. She closed her eyes and willed herself to relax, but she couldn't get her guest out of her mind.

She told herself she was foolish. He was a stranger. She knew nothing about him, except what he'd told her. Lies. She was sure of it, though she couldn't figure out why he'd thought lying was necessary. What could a man like Caleb have to hide?

Hurt, bleeding, in pain, he'd trudged through a landslide and a rainstorm to land on her doorstep. Bandaged, yet still in pain, he'd insisted on leaving. To find his friend, he'd said. Because he'd had no choice but to stay, he'd settled down to lend her a sympathetic ear.

Shannon thought about Caleb's concern for his friend. More than once during the evening he'd looked out the window at the unceasing rain, his frustration apparent. She felt bad about having to refuse him transportation. And she didn't like the idea of leaving some poor man out there exposed to the elements. She prayed he'd found refuge like Caleb.

Caleb. What was it about him that drew her to him?

Not just his looks, although those were exceptional. Not just his touch, although her skin had tingled when he'd touched her and her breasts had ached when they'd been pressed against his chest. Not his dimple, although it showed an impish sense of humor in his otherwise hard face.

Shannon opened her eyes to stare at the fire, and saw in the flames images of Caleb's face. What was it about him that made his face so difficult to forget? Something in those beautiful blue eyes… Warmth? Empathy? She didn't know if it was one thing or many. She only knew there was something about him.

Something you have to forget, Shannon. You don't need another man who'll lie to you, for whatever reason. You had enough of that with Tony.

Not for the first time Shannon wondered if maybe Tony's job would have been easier for her to accept if she'd known more about it. Instead, he'd made up stories to keep her from worrying. Tony had been adamant about not bringing his work home with him. After a while he'd hardly brought himself home.

Shannon turned onto her back. An image of Caleb, half-dressed, sitting on this very couch intruded on her thoughts. She groaned and covered her eyes with her hands.

How stupid can you be, Shannon Garrett? Caleb Joseph is a stranger. You'd be nuts to let yourself get involved with him.

She turned to stare again into the dancing flames. "You'd be nuts," she whispered.

Because tomorrow or the next day or the next, Caleb would be gone. And it wouldn't matter at all that she wished he could stay.

"BRANDON, NO!"

A vehement cry startled Shannon out of a light sleep.

"Dammit, Brandon, answer me!"

Caleb, she realized. He must be having a nightmare. She pushed back the quilt and swung her feet to the floor. The clock over the mantel chimed two. She'd checked him about an hour before, and he'd been sleeping peacefully.

She got up and padded on bare feet into the bedroom. Caleb had kicked off the covers and was thrashing around on the bed, moaning. Her heart went out to him. It was obvious his ordeal hadn't just been physical.

She went over to the side of the bed and spoke to him quietly. "Wake up, Caleb."

Gently she touched his left arm, but he grabbed her hand, staring at her with unseeing eyes. "Where's Brandon? I can't find him." The anguish on his face was a testimony to the closeness he shared with the man, whoever he was.

Suddenly he sat bolt upright. "I've got to go find Brandon."

Shannon pushed him firmly back on the bed. "You're not going anywhere."

He didn't fight her, just lay back against the pillows, eyes closed, murmuring. "Brandon…have to find Brandon. I left him…should have stayed."

She touched his forehead, smoothing back his hair in a gentle rhythm. "Quiet now, Caleb. You need to rest. Someone will find your friend. You'll see, he'll be safe and sound." At least she hoped he would. Caleb already hated himself for leaving his friend alone. She could tell him he'd had no choice and he'd done the right thing until she was blue in the face. If something terrible had happened to his friend, she suspected Caleb would never forgive himself.

When he seemed to be sleeping again, Shannon covered him, then backed away from the bed. Careful not to make any noise, she perched on her overstuffed chair and watched him.

Though his breathing came evenly, his expression still showed its earlier distress. The scratches on his face showed no signs of infection, nor did the larger cut at his hairline. The lump on his forehead had started to color, promising to be multihued by morning.

Caleb moaned and turned onto his side. Shannon held her breath until he settled. The movement caused the blanket to shift, baring his chest to his waist. Evidently he'd chosen to wear only the sweatpants she'd given him earlier. The bandage on his upper arm showed white against his tanned skin.

A few more inches to the left and Caleb wouldn't have come into her life at all.

Shannon hugged herself, feeling a chill that had more to do with her morbid thoughts than the coolness of the room.

Caleb moved onto his back, mumbling. "Mick… It was Mick."

Shannon lowered her brows. Mick? That was a new name. She wondered who he was.

"Dammit, Brandon… The case…the bust…was set…. How did they know?" Caleb's words were filled with frustration and confusion.

Shannon held her breath while he spelled out in mumbled words what she'd suspected. What she'd yearned to deny in the face of his smooth lies.

Caleb was a cop.

She'd heard the same emotions in Tony's voice time and time again. Though he'd never told her the details of his cases, he hadn't been able to hide when something was bothering him. He hadn't allowed her to help him, either.

That had only heightened her frustration. She was a person who craved details. That was why she did the column. She could handle anything, if she knew what was going on. Not knowing drove her to distraction.

Caleb had used different tactics. He'd probably even had different reasons, but the results were the same. Once again she'd been lied to. Once again she'd been treated like a child. And soon another man would leave her behind to pick up the pieces.

Another moan from the bed brought her attention back to Caleb. He moved restlessly in his sleep, kicking at the blankets.

"Where's Brandon? Have to find Brandon..."

Shannon moved to his side and touched his shoulder. "Shh, Caleb. Relax. Everything's fine," she soothed. To do anything else when he was so distressed was unthinkable. He might not want her help during his waking hours, but for now he had no choice.

He didn't respond to her voice and, instead, became more agitated. "Where is he? Where is he?" He kicked at the covers. "The other side...have to get to the other side. Can't do it...can't make it. Have to get help."

Shannon grasped his shoulders and shook him. "Wake up, Caleb. It's a dream, just a dream. You have to wake up."

He continued restlessly, first mumbling, then yelling for Brandon until Shannon's heart broke for him. Unable to wake him, she climbed onto the bed and pulled him to her, holding him, murmuring gentle sounds meant to soothe him.

"Hold on, honey, everything's going to be all right."

He seemed to hear her, because his arms went around her and he held on tight.

Shannon didn't know how long they held each other, he mumbling his nightmare thoughts, she whispering soothing words. Finally he relaxed against her and was quiet. By then she knew nearly everything about his ordeal. Piecing together each bit of information he revealed during his restless sleep, she learned the truth he hadn't trusted her with during his waking hours.

And still she held him.

The clock in the living room chimed four before Shannon allowed herself to leave Caleb and return to her couch. She lay under the quilt. Myriad emotions vied for her attention. She thought about Caleb's ordeal and his reaction to it. This was not a cold man. He cared. How could she hold his lies against him when she knew he'd only done it to protect himself, and maybe her?

Because she understood, she was glad she'd been able to help him relax and finally get the peaceful rest he needed to heal.

It was too bad Tony had never allowed her to—

She shut the thought out of her mind. She couldn't keep comparing the two men. It seemed disloyal, especially since she'd just spent two hours lying in bed next to another man.

A man who raised physical sensations in her that she'd thought she'd buried along with her dead husband.

The clock chimed the half hour, and Shannon turned onto her side. Now she knew. Caleb was a cop. And she wanted him more than any man she'd ever known. How was she supposed to handle that?

Who says you have to handle anything? a voice inside her asked. *Tomorrow or the next day he'll be gone. You said it yourself. And things can go back to normal.*

Closing her eyes, she tried to shut out the voice and give in to the exhaustion that bade her sleep. But there was one more question ringing inside her head that refused to go unsaid: What was so great about normal?

Chapter Five

Caleb lay on his back, eyes closed, willing his body to quit hurting. But it soon became clear his will was no match for the aches and pains that had worsened overnight. He felt as if he'd participated in an all-night decathlon.

Raising a hand to his pounding head, he resigned himself to the fact that he was going nowhere right now. Even if Shannon agreed to lend him her Jeep, he was in no shape to drive, especially in a rainstorm.

He knew it shouldn't matter. There was no doubting that his fellow agents would leave no stone unturned in their search for him and Brandon. Why, by now his partner could be safe and sound, the Driscoes could be in custody and the whole disastrous bust could be saved.

And he could be lying between silk sheets in Xanadu.

But he wasn't. The storm that had ravaged the mountains the past eighteen hours would make a safe search nearly impossible. The hillside was unsteady, the rain a constant presence. Their fellow agents would try with everything in them, but his gut told him that a happy ending to this particular disaster was too optimistic.

Something had gone horribly wrong. Something that had to do with the mysterious Mick. And he suspected it was going to take more than wishful thinking to dig the agency out of this pile of cow manure.

The door to the bedroom opened, and Shannon peeked in. When she saw he was awake, she walked into the room, a white bottle in one hand, a glass of water in the other. "I thought you might need some aspirin. You had a hard night. And you always feel worse the next day when you've been injured."

Caleb levered himself up to sit on the side of the bed and watched her walk over to him. Even dressed in faded blue jeans, a thigh-length forest-green sweater and brown fringed moccasins, she moved with a lazy grace he had to admire. She held her head high like a queen. Her long tawny hair bounced around her shoulders as if it had a life of its own. God, she was gorgeous. He could watch her coming and going and never get tired.

"Here." She handed him the glass of water. Then she flipped the lid off the aspirin bottle and shook out two tablets, which she slipped into his hand. "I know you probably need more, but we'll stick to the normal dose, okay?"

"Okay." He put the pills in his mouth, drained the glass of water and handed it back. "Thanks."

She nodded. "No problem. Is there anything else I can do for you?"

Looking at her, her eyes intent, her full mouth curved, a million things came to mind. Not one of them appropriate.

Get a hold of yourself, Carlisle. The lady wasn't

offering herself. Which was just as well, because after the dreams he'd had the night before, he wouldn't have the willpower to say no. And until she knew the truth about him, it wouldn't be fair to allow her to get involved.

"How about the sweatshirt?" she asked, nodding to where it sat on top of the dresser. "It's kind of cold in here."

Funny, he'd thought the same thing before she'd walked into the room. "No, thanks, I have everything I need." Except her, in bed, naked.

Damn! He had to stop thinking that way. She'd taken him into her home, tended his wounds, fed him, given up her bed for him. And he'd lied to her.

It didn't matter that he wanted her in that bed.

Or that she'd already shared the bed with him in his dreams.

First there'd been the nightmare. He'd been searching for Brandon, digging through the landslide's rubble while lightning flashed and thunder boomed. Then Shannon had come. She'd talked to him quietly, reassuring him that his friend would be found safe and sound. She'd held him, laying his pounding head on the cushion of her breasts, soothing him with her gentle hands. The dream was so vivid it was hard to remember it was only a dream. Wishful thinking.

Impossible.

Noticing a faraway look in Shannon's eyes and a pink tinge to her cheeks, Caleb thought for a moment that she was remembering the dream, too.

"Well," she said on a shaky breath, "I think you should put it on, anyway." She got the sweatshirt and handed it to him. "If you don't want anything else,

I'll go and let you get some rest." She turned abruptly and walked to the door.

He watched her go, enjoying the sway of her hips beneath the loose sweater. Poetry in motion. And he wasn't a man who made romantic comparisons. God, he had to get out of here soon or he wouldn't want to leave at all. "Thanks for the aspirin."

She glanced over her shoulder and smiled. "You're welcome." Then she went out, closing the door behind her.

Without her smile to light it, the room cooled and darkened. Caleb shook his head at his fanciful thought, but he couldn't shake off the truth of it. Something about Shannon Garrett drew him more than any other woman he'd known. The vulnerability under the confident façade? The kindness under the cool practicality? The secrets that hid in the depths of her green eyes?

All of the above, he thought. And more.

He put on the sweatshirt and lay back on the pillows and closed his eyes. Immediately an image of Shannon, cool grace and lush femininity, implanted itself on his brain. Her tall slender body had the twin pleasures of softness and strength that made him want to dive in, not caring in the least if he drowned.

A warmth pulsed through his body, relaxing him. His limbs felt heavy. Thinking about Shannon, he let himself drift off to sleep.

Twelve chimes from the clock in the living room woke him later. The extra few hours of rest had eased the hammer blows in his head. He got up and peeled off the sweatshirt Shannon had lent him.

In the dim natural light of the bathroom, Caleb checked his own clothes. Shannon had rinsed out his jeans and shirt and hung them on a line in the bathtub, but they were still wet.

He washed up with the bottled water Shannon had left on the counter. The cool water felt good. He grabbed a towel from a hook and dried off, then went back into the bedroom.

He glanced out the window and saw the rain hadn't slackened. Though it was just noon, the room was nearly dark. He made his way over to the oak dresser and lit the oil lamp Shannon had left there.

There was a tap on the door, then it opened. Shannon stuck her head in. "I thought I heard you moving around. Do you feel better?"

"Yeah, thanks, I do. You were right about me needing some sleep."

"Well, I have some lunch ready for you when you are."

There was a nervous hitch in her voice he wondered about.

"Sure, I'll be right there."

A rumble of thunder sounded.

"It sounds like the storm's still holding on. I thought it would be gone by now."

Shannon grimaced. "This has been an awful winter. I can't remember the last time we saw the sun." She went out, closing the door behind her.

Shannon was the closest thing to sun *he'd* seen in a long time. Caleb put the sweatshirt back on and went out to join her.

She'd made peanut-butter-and-jelly sandwiches. They sat by the fire as they ate, both lost in their own thoughts. When they were done, Shannon took their plates to the kitchen area.

She returned a few minutes later, looking as if she

had something she wanted to say. Caleb knew he could just stay silent, not ask her what was bothering her; he'd already allowed himself to become too involved with his mysterious hostess. But something made him speak.

"What's on your mind, Shannon?"

"Nothing, it's just…"

"What?" He'd come to expect her to be more straightforward when she had something to say.

She sat on the couch near him. "You had a couple of nightmares last night."

"I'm not surprised. I appreciate you watching over me."

She flushed. "It was no problem," she said brusquely. "Anyway, mostly you were concerned about Brandon."

He nodded. "Yes, my par…uh, pal. He was on the other side of a stream when the landslide hit." He stopped at the strange look on her face. As the saying went, the jig was up. "You know, don't you."

"That you really are a cop? Yes."

"Look, I'm sorry I had to lie. It was for your safety, as well as mine. If the wrong person comes looking for me, you'd be safer if you could honestly tell them you didn't know anything."

Her expression held no censure. "I understand, Caleb." She frowned. "That is your real name, isn't it?"

"Caleb Joseph Carlisle," he supplied. "I'm an undercover agent with the Special Drug Unit of the Santa Cruz County Sheriff's Department."

She nodded. "I figured as much. The SDU has been a visible presence in the area for quite a while."

She paused. "Caleb, during your second nightmare you started talking about someone named Mick."

He raised his brows. Mick. Dammit, who was he and what did he have to do with the fiasco yesterday?

"Did you have another agent out there with you?"

"Just Brandon," he said. "The other agents were waiting for our signal. Brandon and I had been working on this undercover drug operation for months. Everything had been planned." He scowled, remembering. "Then it blew up in our faces."

"So Mick was one of the drug dealers?"

Caleb shrugged. "We don't know *who* he is. We only know that by the time Brandon and I arrived, the Driscoe brothers knew we were cops. Jim Driscoe told his brother to get a hold of Mick as Bran and I were trying to get away."

"So the Driscoes are the drug dealers you were after."

"Yeah," Caleb said. Normally he wouldn't have discussed a case with a civilian, but since he'd already spilled most of the details in his sleep, there didn't seem to be any reason not to. Talking to Shannon helped him to form an image in his own mind of what had happened. Maybe it would help him figure out what went wrong. "Jim, Henry, and J.P. Driscoe have one of the biggest cocaine operations around. And they seemed to be partial to teenagers as customers."

Her green eyes darkened. "Greedy bastards."

Caleb agreed. The Driscoe brothers were scum, and in spite of his current injuries, he wasn't going to stop until they were brought down. "Which is why I have to leave soon, Shannon. I know you're worried about my driving your Jeep, but these men are merciless."

And if they followed him here and hurt her, he'd never forgive himself.

A bright flash of light illuminated the room, followed immediately by a loud crack, then breaking glass.

"Get down!" Caleb pushed her to the floor, threw himself on top of her and reached automatically for a gun that wasn't there.

Thunder boomed, shaking the cabin.

Shannon's heart pounded as Caleb's bulk kept her pinned to the floor. What had caused him to react to the thunder like that? Could he be having some kind of flashback? "Caleb, what are you doing?"

Caleb covered her mouth with his hand. "Shh."

She pushed him again to no avail, then tried to wriggle from under him.

"Cut that out!"

His whispered order tickled her ear. She did what he said, but only because moving against him was making things worse. It had set her blood on fire. Her breasts had melted against him. Her arms ached to pull him closer.

Using both hands, she tried to pry his hand from her lips.

Suddenly her mouth was free. "What are you doing?" she whispered back, though she didn't know why.

"Didn't you hear glass breaking? I think it was a rifle shot."

Shannon's heart stopped for a second. Someone was shooting at her cabin? "It's pouring rain out there. Why would anyone be shooting a rifle in the middle of a storm?"

She saw the answer on his face. "You think someone followed you here?"

He looked down at her. "I don't know. But I'm not taking any chances."

Chances? She was taking a chance staying here, his body covering hers. His lips were so close, she felt his breath on her own lips. It took more willpower than she thought she possessed not to kiss him then and there.

"Shannon, listen to me."

She looked into his eyes. Even in the firelight, she could see how seriously he was taking the situation. "I'm listening."

"I need you to stay absolutely still. I'm going to lift my head a little and look around."

She nodded.

Caleb lifted his head and scanned the room, then lowered himself back down.

"Did you see anything?"

He shook his head. "The couch is in the way." He paused for a moment. "I'm going to have to leave you here."

The very thought frightened her. What if there really was a gunman out there? What if he was shot again? "No!" She grabbed his sweatshirt. "Stay here."

"I can't."

His voice was soothing, reminding her that he'd been in this kind of situation many times. She tried to resent it, to believe he was being reckless just like Tony. But she was sensible enough to know the difference between Tony's need to be first at the scene and Caleb's need to protect them both.

"All right, then," she said reluctantly, "but be careful."

"That's my girl." He kissed her full on the lips.

She barely had time to react before he levered himself off her. Moving cautiously, he raised his head so he could see beyond the sofa.

Shannon held her breath.

Lightning flashed.

Thunder rolled.

And Caleb started to laugh.

Gripping his sweatshirt with both hands, Shannon pulled him down beside her. "What are you laughing at?"

"A branch!" he explained when he could finally get his breath. "A bolt of lightning must have hit a tree outside your kitchen window."

It took a moment for Shannon to take in that what might have been a gunman stalking Caleb had only been a branch striking and smashing the window above her sink. Then all she could say was, "Thank God."

The fear that had balled up inside her broke through, releasing a flood of tears. She put her hands to her face.

"Shannon? Are you crying?"

Without waiting for an answer, Caleb turned her into his arms and held her. He rubbed his hands on her back as she wept, whispering soothing sounds in her ear.

Lying on the floor, cuddled against his strong body, Shannon had never felt so safe. She put her arms around him and held on. "I was so scared. I thought someone had come after you."

Caleb had never been so touched. Shannon hadn't

been afraid for herself. She'd only been worried about him.

He tightened his arms around her. "I'm sorry I frightened you." He rubbed her back. "Everything's okay now."

She leaned back and looked up at him. Firelight cast a glow on her face. Even awash with tears, it was the loveliest face he'd ever seen. But he wanted to see her smile again. She'd had enough pain in her life.

He lowered his head and brushed his lips against her soft cheek. Then he began to kiss the tears away. When he touched the corner of her mouth, Caleb knew he had to taste her or go mad.

But he had no right.

Reluctantly he loosened his hold on her and moved back. He'd go tend the shattered window in the kitchen.

"No." Shannon reached up her hand, threaded her fingers through his hair and pulled him back. "Don't stop."

And she kissed him.

The fire that had been smoldering deep inside Caleb flared to life. It burned in his blood. A fever only Shannon could cure. He ran his hands over her body, knowing he could never have enough. He devoured her mouth, hungry for its unique flavor.

He tasted salt. He tasted sweet lemon. He tasted Shannon, and still he wanted more.

Her hands went under his shirt, nails grazing his skin, igniting flame after flame.

She pushed at the material. "Take it off." The impatient request against his lips demanded obedience.

He stripped off the sweatshirt, then reached for her.

''No, wait.'' She tugged off her own sweater. She wasn't wearing a bra.

For a moment all he could do was stare. She had the most beautiful breasts he'd ever seen. High, full, round, with a satiny texture his fingers ached to explore. He reached out and thumbed a pale pink nipple. It puckered at his touch.

Caleb raised his gaze to Shannon's and saw his own need reflected in her eyes. ''I want you.''

She came into his arms with sweet generosity. Her breasts flattened against his chest, and her lips melted under his kiss. The wide full mouth that had fascinated him since he'd first seen her opened for his tongue.

He dipped and probed, exploring every inch of her velvety mouth, expecting to be satisfied, then finding he wanted more. The fire in his loins burned with intense heat. Too hot, too soon. He wanted to take his time.

He took his lips from hers and was rewarded with a tiny moan of protest. ''It's all right, honey. I'm not going far.''

He backed up his reassurance immediately, placing tiny kisses down the sensitive skin of her neck. Shivers of desire flowed through Shannon. The dreams that had disturbed her sleep had been wonderful, but they didn't begin to compare to the real thing.

Caleb's hands were a miracle. Big, hard, roughened a little with calluses, they traced a path over her back, her waist, her breasts, setting her ablaze. She felt exquisitely tortured, yet totally protected. When his fingers released the snap of her jeans, she wondered only why it had taken so long.

He lowered the zipper, then caressed her through

her silky panties. Even that flimsy layer of material put too much between them. She arched closer, needing more. "Take them off. Please."

Caleb stripped off her jeans and panties in one motion. But instead of returning to the point of her pleasure, he lowered his mouth to her breasts. His tongue circled each nipple until they were hard, then he teased them with his lips until she thought she'd burst into flame.

She pushed her fingers through his dark hair and tried to pull him closer. He resisted. Momentarily. Then he swooped down on one sensitive nipple, taking it with a possessiveness that made her cry out with rapture.

Her body pulsed with unfulfilled ecstasy. Knowing what she needed, she reached down to touch him. She felt his hardness through the sweatpants. The fire in her blood demanded urgency. Putting her fingers on his waistband, she pushed the pants down over his buttocks.

He left her for a moment to kick them off, then he returned. His hands seems to be everywhere, touching her, pleasuring her, creating a need she could never have imagined. His legs tangled with hers, the rough hardness chafing her own smooth length. Yet she felt only bliss.

Then his mouth was once again on hers, sweetly demanding everything she was willing to give. She gave, then demanded in return. And he gave. Fire for fire. Possession for possession. Need for need.

She felt his hardness push against her belly and knew just kissing him would never be enough. She dragged her mouth from his and nipped at his ear.

"I want you inside me. Now. I need you so."

He raised himself above her, pushing a knee between her thighs. Then he did no more.

She looked up and found herself caught in the deep pools of his eyes. "Caleb?"

"Are you sure, Shannon?"

Shannon gazed into the intense melting blue of his eyes. Somewhere inside her fevered body she knew that she was taking a life-changing risk. If she gave herself to him, she would no longer be able to run back to her little cocoon. Nothing would ever be the same again.

Then she thought of the emotions Caleb had dragged out of her lonely frozen body ever since he'd landed on her doorstep, and there was no doubt. She wanted this man. She had never been surer of anything in her life.

She pulled his head down and kissed him deeply. When she released him, she could hardly breathe, she wanted him so much.

She opened herself to him. *"Yes."*

He gazed down at her with a tenderness that made her heart leap. He entered her with exquisite slowness. Need coursed through her, and she arched to meet him.

He filled her.

Then he began to move against her with a leisurely rhythm that drove her to the edge. She grasped his hips, digging in her nails. "More, Caleb. Please more."

He surged against her, his passion making her gasp. Again and again he drove toward her velvety center.

Still it wasn't enough. Shannon wrapped her legs around him. "Closer. Harder." And still the flames inside her grew.

Caleb had never known such response from a woman. She was like a fiery whirlpool, drawing him in. Her nails dug into his back, urging him on. The heat in his loins raged, burning like a bonfire. He ached for release. And still he went on. Pleasuring Shannon, kissing her, touching her, giving all of himself. Plunging into the generous folds of her body.

Until she cried out her joy.

Only then did he allow his own surrender to the explosive power of their union.

Chapter Six

Caleb awoke to the flickering light of an oil lamp on the bedside table and the sound of a clock chiming five. When the chime ceased, the cabin seemed eerily silent. The rain had stopped, he realized.

Shannon lay next to him on the bed, her head resting on his left shoulder. She moved in her sleep, cuddling against him. He gazed down at her face. Her dark thick lashes shadowed her high cheekbones. Her face looked softer in sleep, without the anger and hurt that had sharpened her features. His heart swelled a little with pride that he was the one who had put that relaxed look on her face.

Her hair lay in silky ribbons on her bare shoulders. He found the subtle glow of her skin tantalizing and reached out to touch it. The movement sent a flash of pain through his arm, soon forgotten as his fingers caressed Shannon's soft skin. A healing warmth spread through him.

How strange, he thought, that the disastrous circumstances of the day before had led him to this lovely woman. It was a shame he had to wake her from such peaceful sleep to tell her goodbye.

He shifted, catching his breath as a fire erupted in

his injured ankle. It didn't matter. It couldn't. Just like Shannon's feelings, whatever they might be, couldn't matter right now. He had to find his partner.

A vision of the slide flashed in his mind. Tons of rock and mud roaring toward them, the ground shaking, lightning flashing, thunder booming. He'd been able to escape the onslaught. Had Brandon?

Caleb's head pounded at the thought that he might have lost his partner and best friend in a bust gone bad. He closed his eyes, willing away the negative bent his mind had chosen to take. This wasn't getting him anywhere.

He had a job to do. He'd indulged his injuries long enough. While the storm had continued unabated, he'd had to accept his forced inactivity. Now it was time for him to get back to the real world. The Driscoes had made them. And it wasn't because the three moron brothers had suddenly developed brains. Someone else had discovered his and Brandon's identity. But who?

Boom, boom, boom!

Caleb started as someone pounded on the wooden front door.

"Ms. Garrett? Shannon? Are you there?" a male voice called out.

The man knocked again.

Caleb threw back the covers and moved gingerly to sit on the edge of the bed.

"Who the heck?" Grasping the quilt to her bare breasts, Shannon sat up.

Caleb stood. "Stay here. I'll go see who it is." He only wished he had his weapon to take with him.

He limped soundlessly into the living room, where he bent to pick up the sweatpants Shannon had loaned him. He put them on and grabbed a flashlight as the man began pounding on the door again.

Shannon walked into the room, zipping up a turquoise terry-cloth robe. She looked tousled and sweet and much too vulnerable. Caleb's protective instincts kicked into gear. "I told you to stay in the bedroom."

"It's my house," she replied calmly.

Caleb shook his head impatiently. "That's no reason to put your life on the line."

"Ms. Garrett? Are you all right?" the man called out.

She moved to the door. "Doesn't sound like a serial killer to me."

Caleb moved quickly, covering her hand on the iron doorknob with his. "Last I heard, serial killers don't announce themselves. It doesn't hurt to be cautious."

"Who's there?" Caleb raised his voice so the other man could hear him. "What do you want?"

"It's Harvey Moran from PG&E," came the answer. "Who are you? Is Ms. Garrett there?"

Shannon let out a sigh of relief, indicating she wasn't as impervious to the idea of danger as she'd let on. "Go ahead and open the door. I know him."

Caleb narrowed his eyes. "Are you sure?"

She nodded, and he turned on the flashlight and opened the door.

Ever cautious, Caleb shined the light on the visitor. The man on the front porch wore a brown uniform with a Pacific Gas and Electric logo on the front pocket. He looked to be in his fifties, with graying dark hair and laugh lines creasing his concerned face. Concern turned to confusion. "Who are you?" he demanded. "Where's Ms. Garrett?"

Shannon moved to stand in front of Caleb. "I'm right here, Harvey," Shannon said soothingly. "This is my friend Caleb." She glanced back at him, warning in her expression. "Caleb, this is Harvey Moran. He and his wife, Marta, live down the road a few miles."

Harvey nodded, but his gaze didn't stray from Caleb and his frown didn't ease. "I was out checking for downed lines and thought it would be a good idea to come by here. A storm like this, anything could happen."

Shannon smiled. "Thanks for thinking of me, but I'm just fine. I've had company through the worst of it."

Caleb was grateful she hadn't revealed that he was a cop.

Harvey smiled shyly. "Actually I did it for my own protection. Marta said she'd boil me alive if I didn't come by and see if Miss Know-It-All was okay. She can't get through a day without reading your piece in the paper."

Miss Know-It-All? The name had a familiar ring, Caleb thought. Then he remembered. It was a syndicated column, placed in newspapers all over the country. Well, that explained the state-of-the-art computer. He thought of what Shannon had gone through with her husband's death. Reading Miss Know-It-All's informative and amusing columns, he never would have guessed she'd turned herself into a hermit.

He looked at Shannon with new eyes. It must have been hard keeping up appearances when she'd been in so much pain. So she'd hidden herself in a mountain forest, never letting on to her readers that she'd suffered a personal tragedy.

"I don't know why we're talking out here. You must be freezing, Harvey. Why don't you come in? I'll put on some coffee."

Harvey looked at Caleb again. There was speculation in his gaze and not a little suspicion. Caleb didn't blame him. Seeing a strange man at Shannon's cabin, he would have felt the same. Especially since he probably looked a little worse for wear. He decided to put the man at ease.

"Coffee sounds great to me." He smiled at Harvey. "Please join us."

Harvey gave a short nod. "This was my last stop on the way home. I guess it won't hurt to stay a few minutes."

The three of them went into the cabin. Shannon set about making the coffee, while the two men sat at the table.

"So have the downed lines been repaired?" Caleb asked. "Shouldn't the cabin have power?" He didn't want to leave Shannon alone without electricity. He didn't want to leave Shannon at all.

"Should be on any minute," Harvey told them just as the lights flashed on.

The three of them laughed in surprise.

Harvey grinned. "I couldn't have timed it better if I tried. Let there be light."

While they waited for their coffee, Caleb grilled Harvey for whatever information he had about storm damage and the landslide.

Shannon brought over a tray with three cups. "I hope you don't mind instant."

Caleb smiled. "I wouldn't recognize it any other way."

Shannon returned his smile, and once again he was caught in the spell of her eyes. The thought of leaving her behind while he finished his business with the Driscoes hit him in the gut like a one-two punch.

Harvey cleared his throat. "Well, thanks for the coffee, folks. But I really should go home to let Marta know you're all right."

The three of them stood. At the door Shannon gave Harvey a kiss on the cheek. "Thanks again, and tell Marta to quit worrying."

"I will. Have a nice evening, folks."

Caleb watched the older man walk down the steps. Then an idea hit. Damn, why hadn't he thought of this the minute the PG&E man had shown up? "Wait, Harvey!"

Harvey turned to look at him. "Need something?"

"I was wondering if you could give me a ride down the mountain?"

Harvey's gaze went from him to Shannon and back. "You're leaving?"

Caleb was sorry to see the suspicious look return, but there was nothing he could do about that, short of telling the man his business. Something an undercover agent simply could not do.

"I have some stuff to take care of and don't want to leave Shannon without transportation."

Harvey glanced at Shannon. A strange look passed between them. Then Harvey shrugged. "Sure, no problem. I'll wait for you in the truck."

"Thanks," Caleb said. "Just give me a minute to get some clothes on and make a phone call."

"Afraid you won't be able to do that," Harvey

said. "We got all the power lines back in order, but the phone guys are still working on theirs. A mudslide took out several telephone poles a couple miles from here."

Caleb didn't like the idea of going back to the compound blind, but he didn't see how he had a choice.

"Guess my call will have to wait." Caleb went into the cabin.

Shannon followed, closing the door behind her. She didn't ask questions, didn't say a thing. She just watched him with those mysterious eyes of hers.

He pulled on the sweatshirt she'd lent him, then went into the bathroom for his shoes. When he reentered the bedroom, she handed him a pair of thick white tube socks.

"They might be a little snug, but they'll keep your feet from freezing in those damp boots."

Her voice was tight, strained.

He felt a flash of regret. "I have to go."

"I know," she replied softly. Her eyes were unreadable.

Explanations didn't come easily to him, but he felt the need now. "I have to find out what happened to Brandon."

"I understand." She turned away and started straightening the quilts on the bed.

She understood, he thought, the taste of it a little bitter on his tongue. Of course she understood. She'd been through all this before with her husband. The leave-takings, the explanations, the injuries, the promises to return. Until the day he hadn't come back.

"I'm not him, Shannon."

She swung around to glare at him, wordlessly daring him to go on.

As much as his words might hurt her, he knew he had to continue. "I'm not going to do anything reckless. It's been more than twenty-four hours since our aborted bust. The compound will be swarming with cops. They've probably started a house-to-house search. I need to let them know I'm all right. And I need to check on my partner. As soon as I've done that, I'll come back."

"Don't!"

The sharpness of the order silenced him.

She looked away from him. "Don't make promises you can't keep."

Caleb sat on the chair and put on his boots. He didn't blame her for being skeptical. "I'm not saying I'll be back tonight. A snafu like this means tons of paperwork to fill out and lots of debriefing." He tied the laces, then stood. "If the other agents didn't get there in time to arrest Jim and J.P., a manhunt will have to be organized." And then there was Mick. Who was he? How had he known about the bust?

"Caleb, I don't need explanations. I was a cop's wife, remember? I know all about the red tape and the reports." She picked up a pillow, fluffed it and then threw it back on the bed. "And you don't have to worry about what happened between us this afternoon, either."

Caleb watched her move around the bed, fluffing and smoothing as if trying to brush away the vision of the two of them. She wouldn't be able to do it. He wouldn't let her. He strode over and grasped her arm, tugging her around to face him. "Worry about it? No. Think about it? I won't be able to stop doing that. And you won't, either."

Before she could deny it, he pulled her against him and kissed her hard.

She could have resisted. She could have pushed him away, slapped his face in outrage.

She didn't do any of those things.

Instead, Shannon gave as good as she got, kissing him with a fervor that fanned his barely banked desire into a raging inferno. There was no doubt she wanted him. And God knew, he wanted her.

The last thing he wanted to do was leave her alone right now. But a relationship started at the expense of others was no relationship at all.

Gathering every bit of strength he had, Caleb pushed Shannon away.

Their breathing sounded harsh in the silent cabin. He gazed at her face, regretting deeply the chill of abandonment in her eyes. "I'll be back, Shannon."

She nodded, but there was nothing positive in it.

Knowing there was nothing else he could say, Caleb turned and left the room.

SHANNON STOOD at the door and watched Caleb walk to the truck. She wanted to tell him to be careful, to watch his back, to return soon, to somehow come up with the right combination of words that would bring him back safely. In the end she said nothing. There were no words to stop a cop from doing his duty at the risk of his own life. And the lives of others.

She immediately clamped down on the thought. Tony hadn't known. Neither had she.

Until it was too late.

She waited until the truck's taillights disappeared into the gloom before closing the door. Restlessly she went from room to room, not really sure what to do with herself. Everywhere she looked were reminders of Caleb's stay. The dishes in the sink, his damp clothes still hanging in the bathroom. She'd straightened the bed earlier, but a vision of the two of them lying on the rumpled covers after making love, wouldn't leave her. The man had been in her cabin only twenty-four hours, yet he'd imprinted himself on her refuge as if he'd been there for years.

She reached out a hand to touch the pillow where his head had lain not a half hour before. A lingering warmth teased her fingertips.

She jerked away from the bed and almost ran from the room. God, how could she have been so stupid? Not only had she made love with a stranger, she'd let herself get involved with a cop. An undercover SDU agent, no less.

She paced from the living room to the kitchen and back again, scolding herself with every step. *Did you really think that making love with him would end your loneliness?* she asked herself. *Well, Shannon, where is he now?*

Hadn't she learned her lesson the first time? Hadn't Tony given her an excellent example of the type of man it was foolish to get involved with? He'd put everything before her and their marriage. His job, his fellow cops, the victims of the crimes he'd investigated and the criminals who'd committed them. Caleb wouldn't be any different.

He might have brought her to life again, but that didn't mean he was going to stay around to see the results. Hadn't he just left her side to go back to the job?

She wasn't being fair. She knew she wasn't. His

partner could be in grave danger. She really did understand why he'd had to leave.

With a sigh Shannon sat on the edge of the couch and stared into the dying embers of the fire. An image of the two of them lying naked on the floor drifted into her mind. The firelight dancing on their skin. The heat rising in her that had nothing to do with the logs burning in the fireplace. She'd never felt so desired, so sensual, so hot. Not even with her husband.

No, Caleb was different from Tony in many ways. She'd even believed him when he said he'd be back. What had happened between them had been so intense it couldn't be ignored. But that didn't mean she took top priority. He would come back—in a day or a week, depending on his job or his partner's health or the state of their investigation.

One day he would drive into her clearing. His hair would be dry this time, dark and springy and still a little long. His eyes would be blue and clear as a mountain stream. He would give her that smile of his, and his dimple would flash to life. And foolish woman that she was, she would be happy to see him.

And absolutely devastated when he left to go back undercover again.

She'd be damned if she was going to put herself through this again. She jumped up and strode to the bedroom. At the closet she retrieved her biggest suitcase and placed it on the bed. Opening her dresser drawers, she began throwing in clothes.

She was not going to sit around waiting for Caleb to decide it was time to check in with her. She'd been cooped up in this cabin long enough. Now that the rain looked as if it was going to hold off for a while, it was the perfect time to go stay in Monterey for a few days. Zoe had been bugging her to visit. "Come on, Shannon," she said the last time they'd talked. "Think of it as a vacation. You haven't had one in years."

And I deserve one, she told herself as she continued packing.

She'd stay at Zoe's house on the beach. Maybe her friend could take some time off from the hospital. They could take walks, shop, go out for dinner, have fun. She was weeks ahead on her columns. She'd been answering other people's questions for years. Now it was time she did something for herself.

Her packing completed, she closed the suitcase and snapped the locks.

And if Caleb came back while she was gone? a little voice interjected.

Shannon tossed her head. "Well, then, he'll just have to wait for me."

THE DRISCOE COMPOUND lay a little less than three miles from the bottom of the long winding lane that led to Shannon's cabin. A shiver went through Caleb when he realized just how close the two properties were. One of the Driscoe brothers could have shown up at Shannon's any time during the past twenty-four hours. Thank God the storm had lengthened the short distance. Impassable roads and raging creeks were a deterrent for even the most vicious of criminals.

"The driveway is just ahead on the left, Harvey. You can let me out here."

Harvey pulled over the truck across from the driveway and stopped. "Do you want to try the cell phone again before you leave?"

Caleb picked it up and dialed, but he doubted it

would do any good. Between the weather and the mountains, the cell phone had proved pretty much useless. This call didn't go through, either, so he switched it off and put the phone back in its holder on the dash.

He reached for the door handle. "Thanks for the ride, Harvey."

"You sure you don't want me to take you up the driveway?" Harvey asked. "I noticed at Ms. Garrett's that you were limping."

Caleb shook his head. The last thing he wanted to do was involve another civilian in this mess. To explain away his injuries, he'd told Harvey that he was visiting friends when he'd been caught in the storm and had to take refuge in Shannon's cabin. "I'll be fine. It isn't far."

Harvey reached behind the seat and retrieved a flashlight. "Well, at least take this. It's dark out there."

He handed the light to Caleb, who had no choice but to take it. To tell the other man that he didn't want to announce his arrival until he got the lay of the land would bring up questions he didn't want to answer.

Caleb got out of the car. "Thanks again, Harvey." He closed the door, then waited until the truck drove off before crossing the street.

The rain had caused rivulets to form in the dirt road. Caleb stepped over one, only to have his foot land on a rock. His ankle turned, sending a streak of pain up his leg. He uttered a string of profanities under his breath.

Ankle on fire, he started off again. It wasn't easy, but every time he got the urge to stop, he thought of

Brandon. The man wasn't just his partner; he was his friend. He had to be all right.

What seemed like hours later, but was probably only twenty minutes, he caught sight of the compound. There were several cars in the clearing—two sheriff's vehicles, the truck he and Brandon had driven up in and two sedate-looking sedans he recognized as belonging to fellow SDU agents.

He stopped to catch his breath. If there were that many cops in the area, they must still be looking for someone. Him, certainly. Brandon? Had he been buried under the slide? If they'd suspected so, wouldn't there have been a rescue squad around?

Henry Driscoe had been killed before the slide. How much had his brothers cared about him? Would they have left him to rot on the rain-sodden hillside? Or had they stuck around long enough for the other agents to apprehend them?

Caleb pressed his hands to his temples. Standing in the dank woods wasn't going to get his questions answered. But it had made his headache return full force, dammit. He sure hoped one of the guys had some aspirin.

He saw the captain, Sean Gallagher, walk out of the Driscoes' barn, accompanied by a Santa Cruz County Sheriff's deputy. Caleb was glad to see Gallagher. He'd taken over as captain just after Caleb had joined the SDU, and Caleb respected his abilities as an investigator. If anyone could figure out who Mick was, it was Gallagher.

Caleb gave a long low whistle that he knew the older man would recognize. Then he put his hands over his head and continued down the driveway into the compound. He wasn't taking any chances on a trigger-happy sheriff's deputy mistaking him for one of those drug-dealing scum. The beefy man standing next to Gallagher looked just the type.

"That you, Carlisle?"

"It's me, Captain Gallagher." Caleb limped forward slowly. His ankle threatened to give out under him, but he kept moving.

Gallagher spoke to the other officer. "The last man's been accounted for. Signal to the others. Then put a call on the radio."

The deputy brought a whistle to his lips and blew three times long and loud, and three times short.

Gallagher moved forward to meet Caleb. "You can put your hands down, Caleb. You don't look too good."

Caleb didn't doubt it. "It's been a long twenty-four hours."

A strange expression crossed the other man's face. But Caleb didn't bother to question it. He had more important things on his mind. "I heard you tell the deputy everyone had been accounted for. Does that mean you found Brandon? Is he all right?"

The deputy strode forward, grabbed Caleb's right arm and twisted it behind his back.

Pain racked Caleb's injured arm. "What the hell?" The next thing he knew he was in cuffs. "Captain, tell this ape who I am!"

The "ape" lowered his ugly face to glare at Caleb. "I know who you are, Carlisle. You're the bastard who shot his partner in the back and left him to die."

Chapter Seven

Confusion and outrage, mixed with concern for his partner, rendered Caleb speechless.

Taking advantage of his silence, the deputy loaded him none too gently into one of the unmarked cars. Captain Gallagher slid his six-four, 250-pound bulk in beside him. Sims and Scatini got into the front seat. Scatini started the car and drove out of the compound.

Caleb looked over at the man next to him. His captain's normally genial face was darkened by a glowering frown. They'd worked together out of the Santa Cruz office a long time. Caleb knew him as a man who laughed easily and enjoyed life to the hilt. Something wasn't right.

"All right, Captain, you want to tell me what the hell is going on? I didn't shoot Brandon Everly, and you know it."

Gallagher glanced at him, his face closed tight as a bank's safe on a Saturday night, then looked away.

Frustration made Caleb want to kick something, but he kept his voice calm as he addressed the men in the front seat. "What about you guys? You wanna tell me why I'm shackled and in custody, while the Driscoes are running around scot-free?"

An unreadable looked passed between the two men.

"Or maybe they aren't," Caleb said, disgust coloring his words. "Maybe you got Jim and J.P. and they've been telling stories."

He'd lost his gun in the slide. Had one of them found it and used it to shoot Brandon? He wouldn't put it past the scum to try to blame him for their dirty work. Surely his fellow agents didn't believe a bunch of charges trumped up by those drug-sucking bums.

Shot and left to die—that was what the deputy had said. Did that mean...? "Is Bran alive?"

Nobody answered.

Caleb focused on the man next to him. "He's my partner, Captain. I need to know."

Gallagher looked away from him. "We'll tell you what you need to know when you need to know it."

Pretty obscure, Caleb thought, and probably as much as he was going to get out of the agent. Under the wide smile, Sean Gallagher always played his cards close to the vest. It was what made him a good agent.

In spite of it, Caleb chose to hope Brandon was still alive. They'd been partners and friends for too many years for him to accept anything else.

Knowing he wasn't going to get any answers now, Caleb stared out the window at the redwood trees they passed as the car wound down the mountain road back to civilization. The deep green of the forest reminded him of Shannon's eyes, so full of secrets, yet so inviting.

Until he'd tried to convince her that he'd return.

Considering the situation he suddenly found himself in, he guessed it was just as well she hadn't believed him.

CALL TO ZOE MADE, bags packed and stowed in the back of the Jeep, Shannon took one more pass through the cabin to make sure windows were latched and the plywood board she and Caleb had used to cover the broken pane in the kitchen window was watertight. The clock on the mantel dinged seven as she closed the front door.

Exactly twenty-four hours since Caleb had landed on her doorstep, she thought as she walked down the steps. Just one day, yet it had turned her life upside down.

Letting herself into the Jeep, she remembered the little wrangle she'd had with Caleb over his taking her vehicle. She wondered what he'd say when he found out that she had an automatic four-wheel-drive truck in the garage the whole time. Would he understand her concern for him, or would he be like Tony, angry that she had made that decision, any decision, without consulting him?

And what did it matter, anyway? They had no future together. He was a cop. She was the widow of a cop. If she ever got involved with a man again, she would make sure he had a job that would bring him home to her and, please God, their children every day.

She drove down her gravel driveway. The entrance to her drive still had some water flowing across, but not enough to impede her escape. She laughed humorlessly at the thought. Three years ago she had run to these hills, hoping to escape the grief and anger that threatened to engulf her when she'd lost first Tony, and then their baby. Twenty-four hours ago she thought she'd gained some peace of mind. No, that wasn't quite true. She *knew* she'd finally come to terms with the past. Now she was running away from her refuge. And she had to wonder if it was really the right thing to do.

She turned onto the narrow lane that wound its way down the mountain. She drove slowly. Experience had taught her that this road was dangerously slippery during the winter. She pushed her doubts to the back of her mind. Once she got to Zoe's, she would talk it out with her friend. For now, she'd better concentrate on her driving.

Glad the rain had stopped for a while, Shannon took the curves cautiously. In the beam of her head-lights, she could see the swollen creek that followed the road. A car passed, going the other way.

Shannon shook her head. "You have to be nuts to be out on the road on a night like this," she said aloud.

Maybe she could use that as an excuse the next time she saw Caleb, plead temporary insanity. Why else would she have gone to bed with a perfect stranger?

Aside from the fact he *was* perfect? A little voice taunted. That gorgeous smile, that charming dimple, that body, so big, so tough, and yet so tender. And those eyes, so clear, so blue, so full of promises.

"Snap out of it, Shannon," she ordered herself. His eyes, his kisses, his touch might have been full of promises, but they were promises he couldn't keep. *He's a cop. No, not just a cop, an undercover SDU agent. Danger in his life. You suffered enough heart-break the last time. How much punishment are you willing to take?*

A light flashed in her eyes. A car had driven up behind her, its headlights reflecting off her rearview mirror. "Back off, buddy," she muttered. "You're way too close for these road conditions."

The car only seemed to creep closer.

Shannon focused on the road ahead. There were no streetlights in the mountains. Only the dark forest, shielded from any moonlight by the thick clouds.

She looked in the mirror again. The other car was right on her tail. Why didn't this guy give her some space? It never ceased to amaze her how stupid some drivers could be.

She reached a straightaway. Good, she thought, maybe the idiot would pass her.

As if he'd heard her, the car pulled into the other lane. It accelerated until it was even with her Jeep.

Shannon glanced over. It was a two-toned sedan, its colors indistinguishable in the darkness. The driver appeared to be a man, his face lit eerily by the green glow from the dash. No passenger that she could see. A chill went through her. She shook it off. "You're being silly, Shannon. He's probably just some guy in a hurry to get home after a long commute."

As if to prove her right, the car sped up.

"See?" she told herself. "The idiot was just passing your car."

Suddenly the sedan swerved toward her.

Shannon pulled the Jeep to the right to avoid it, then jammed on the brake. She assumed the driver had just been avoiding some nocturnal animal, but figured it was best to give him some room.

The other car took off, its taillights soon disappearing into the gloom.

Shannon breathed a little easier. With intense concentration she focused on her driving. The last thing she needed tonight was some jerk deciding that the wet mountain road was the place to try out his skills as a race-car driver.

Her headlights picked up a raccoon scampering across the road. Shannon slowed, letting her gaze wander to the side of the road. Often one animal was followed by another. A distance ahead, something caught her eye. A little flash of red.

Probably a reflector tacked to a tree at the entrance of somebody's driveway, she thought. But as she got closer, she heard the revving of an engine, then her headlights reflected off a car on the side of the road. The same two-toned sedan.

"Hmm. That'll teach him not to—"

Suddenly the car pulled out directly into her path. She slammed on the brakes, but her tires skidded on the wet pavement. She held firmly to the wheel as the Jeep fishtailed, then stopped with a shudder on the opposite side of the road.

Shannon's heart raced. "Maniac!" she cried as the car disappeared around the next corner.

Running shaking hands through her hair, Shannon took a couple of deep breaths.

A van drove up beside her and a young man, a teenager probably, with long bleached-blond hair rolled down his window. "Are you all right, lady?"

She rolled her window down, too, and told him she was fine.

"I saw what that car did to you. Man, the dude must be on crack. I tried to see the license plate, but it was, like, covered with mud. Sorry."

She smiled. "It's okay. Thanks for stopping."

"No problem, lady. Why don't you see if you can get your car back on the road? I'll wait to make sure."

Thanking him again, Shannon eased the Jeep back onto the road, then gave the driver of the van a friendly wave. As she drove off, she noticed that he, too, pulled onto the road and was following her at a comfortable distance.

Shannon smiled, feeling much calmer knowing he was behind her. Even though the guy who'd run her off was probably long gone, it made her feel better not to be alone. It was times like this that made her wonder what she'd thought was so great about being a recluse. Maybe Zoe was right. Maybe it was time to let herself out of her cage.

But that didn't mean she was changing her mind about Caleb Carlisle. It might have taken a while, but she'd learned her lesson. Theirs was one relationship she was ending before it began.

"SO, YOU'D NEVER MET this woman before?"

"No," Caleb said for the third—or was it the fourth?—time.

He shifted on the hard wooden chair. His butt was getting numb sitting in the drab little interrogation room where they'd escorted him upon his arrival at headquarters some three hours ago.

The chair was no more uncomfortable than when he'd been the interrogator, but everything else about this nightmare was totally different. How had this happened? Why was he being treated like a criminal? And by the friends and colleagues he thought he knew, who he thought knew him? At least one of the cops had told him that, indeed, Brandon Everly was alive, but in a coma.

"Explain again how you found Ms. Garrett's cabin."

Caleb swallowed the last sip of lukewarm water from the paper cup he'd been given when his throat had gone dry, then patiently recounted what he remembered of his pain-filled journey.

When he'd finished, he stared straight ahead at the drab gray wall, trying hard to keep his temper in check. He was becoming more and more exasperated with this line of questioning. Did his colleagues really think he'd planned this whole thing right down to the part where he'd shown up at Shannon's door?

An image of her, naked, skin glowing in the firelight, invaded his mind, refusing to leave. It was just as well they didn't know how close he and Shannon had gotten during the hours he'd been stuck in her cabin.

"Sure you're not hiding something, Carlisle?"

Caleb glanced at his interrogator. Sid Munoz was the third agent to question him about the incident at the Driscoe compound. This man, like the others, wasn't just a fellow agent, he was a friend. Caleb had often spent time with Sid and his wife and kids. Just last month, in fact, he'd attended Sid's baby daughter's baptism.

All anger drained out of him. He sighed. "Look, Sid, I've already told you and the others all I know. Why don't you tell me what you know. Then maybe I could help. We're wasting precious time that could be spent looking for the real criminals."

The door opened behind him, but he didn't bother to look around. "The Driscoes could be out of the country by now."

"I doubt that very much," Malcolm Knox said with a grim smile as he pulled out a wooden chair and sat across the scarred table from Caleb. "From what I hear, dead men don't do much travelin'."

Caleb focused his gaze on the newcomer. In his early forties, Knox had put in nearly twenty years in law enforcement. Prior to joining the SDU, he'd spent a couple of years in San Diego with the border patrol, then another dozen as a police officer in San José. He had a reputation for being smart and competent, and held the highest arrest record in the state.

But Caleb still didn't know him well enough to know if he was joking. "Are you saying all three of the brothers are dead?"

Instead of answering, Knox looked at Sid. "Your wife called a few minutes ago, Munoz. Something about the baby."

Sid's dark face showed concern. "Is she all right?"

"I'm sure she is," Knox told him. "But if you want to call her, I can take over here."

Sid glanced at Caleb. He looked like he wanted to say something for a moment. But he just shook his head slightly, then left the room.

Caleb hadn't expected anything different. What could he say? Caleb thought. What could any of them say? Men he'd worked with, men he'd trusted with his life, men he'd become friends with, had accused him of shooting his partner in the back. And the worst thing about it was, he really couldn't blame them.

Something had happened up in those shifting hills, something not right. They wanted answers. Well, so did he.

Knox slid a manila folder across the table toward him.

Caleb picked it up. "What's this?"

"The ballistic report," the agent supplied calmly.

Caleb flipped back the cover and read the single sheet inside. He looked back at Knox, trying hard not to react to the damning information. "They were killed with bullets from my gun."

The other man nodded. "Look further."

Caleb studied the report and found that his gun had been wiped clean, which meant— "Larkin, it had to be Larkin. Or Mick." Whoever he was.

"Or you could have wiped off your prints yourself, trying to set them up."

Caleb narrowed his gaze at him. "Why would I do that?"

Knox sat back in his chair and crossed his arms over his chest. "How's this scenario sound? In the confusion of the fight, you shot your partner in the back. You panicked, afraid no one would believe it was an accident. You killed the other two, since Henry was already dead, as you say, then wiped the prints and threw away the gun, figuring you could always say you'd lost it in the slide. Larkin or this phantom Mick make good scapegoats."

"Is that what you think happened? Is that what they're all thinking?" The volume of Caleb's voice raised with each question. "Do my twelve years of service mean nothing?"

Agent Knox shrugged. His expression was unreadable.

"What about Shannon Garrett? Do you all think I made her up, too?"

"She's nowhere to be found," Knox said. "Or do you think Larkin got to her, too?"

Fear clutched at Caleb's gut. The very thought of Shannon in the hands of a man who'd possibly killed two men in cold blood terrified him. Caleb realized

Knox was watching him closely and forced himself to relax. It wasn't possible that Larkin or Mick knew about Shannon. If either of them followed him to her cabin, both he and Shannon would have been dead by now. Knox was just using fear as a technique to get him to fess up to Shannon's whereabouts.

But that still didn't tell him where Shannon had gone. "No, Knox, I don't think Larkin or Mick got to her. No one followed me to her cabin that night."

"So where is she?"

"I don't know. The last time I saw her was when I left her cabin around five this evening. She never said anything about leaving." She'd hidden herself in those hills for three years. Why would she leave now? Where would she go? Damn! He hated having to put her welfare in other hands, but if he didn't, she could be heading straight for trouble. "You guys have her license-plate number and the description of her car. Why don't you put out an APB?"

"We have." The agent leaned forward. "Look, Caleb, you and I both know you didn't shoot your partner or the Driscoes. You're too good at your job to have made a mistake like that. But some of the others think you're hiding something."

Caleb glared at him. "Well, then I'll just have to prove that I'm not."

A FINE MIST swirled around Shannon's Jeep as she drove down Highway One through the tiny town of Moss Landing. The thickening fog made it hard to see the road ahead. And the car driving behind her now on the two-lane road didn't help. His high beams were on, which only made matters worse.

The lights reflected off her rearview mirror, and she

squinted against the glare. What the heck had she done to deserve two bad drivers in one night?

The dimmed streetlights of Castroville shone in the distance. Within minutes she took the turnoff for Monterey. Finally, she thought, a multilaned highway. Now the car behind her would be able to pass.

When it stayed behind her, she pressed the accelerator, but the distance between the two vehicles didn't lengthen. Shannon frowned. "Well, if you won't move over, I will." She shifted into the fast lane.

The other car did the same.

Shannon's heart started to pound. What the heck was going on?

Again she put on her blinker and moved back to her original lane.

The other car followed.

Nerves rattled, Shannon thought about the two-toned sedan that had run her off the road earlier. Was it possible the driver had done it on purpose? And now could this guy be following her?

"Don't be ridiculous," she told herself.

But she was informed enough to know it wasn't as farfetched as she tried to convince herself. If some man was stalking her, she wouldn't be the first woman to suffer such creepy behavior.

She glanced in the mirror. The car seemed to have backed off a little, but it still followed. She flashed on the ordeal Caleb had been through. Was it possible that one of the drug dealers had followed him to her cabin and was now coming after her?

"Now, that's farfetched." It was more likely some jerk who thought he was God's gift to women. Seeing the lights of Seaside ahead, Shannon decided to put the person on her tail to the test. If he took the same turnoff, she'd simply lead him to the huge shopping center. It should be fairly easy to lose him in the acres of parking.

Traffic was light, so she was able to wait until the last minute to take the exit. Adrenaline flowed through her as she shot across the lanes. She went down the ramp, taking the left turn at the bottom before she looked in the mirror to see if he had followed.

He hadn't.

Well, that was easy, she thought, not knowing whether to be relieved or embarrassed that she'd even suspected she was being followed. *See, Shannon, this is what you get from hanging out with a cop. Paranoia. You're much better off without him.*

Making a U-turn, she returned to the on-ramp and got back on the freeway. The next time she exited, several cars were behind her, but she didn't think any of them was her imagined stalker. Within minutes she arrived at the hospital where Zoe worked. Explaining that the doctor had an emergency and would be home as soon as she could, the receptionist gave her the key to Zoe's house.

It was just as well, Shannon thought as she headed out to the Jeep. Between her nearly sleepless night and her eventful drive, she didn't have the energy for a heartfelt discussion tonight. Tomorrow morning she'd be more capable of withstanding Zoe's barrage of questions.

As she unlocked the car door, Shannon noticed a two-toned sedan parked with others in a dark section of the hospital parking lot. She couldn't see anyone in the car, but that didn't ease her jangled nerves. She hurriedly climbed into the Jeep and started the ignition.

She drove out of the parking lot, keeping one eye on her rearview mirror. No one followed, but it was another few blocks before she could allow herself to relax. By the time she let herself into Zoe's house, she'd convinced herself that the incident in the mountains had colored her imagination. All she needed was a good night's sleep and she'd be fine.

SHANNON HEARD little cooing sounds coming from the crib and smiled. The baby was awake. She walked over and gazed down at her beautiful child. She lowered the side, then bent over and picked up the baby. "It's about time you woke up, sweetie. I thought you were going to sleep all day." Hugging the little bundle to her, she walked out of the room. "We'd better go see your daddy. He's been waiting forever to hold his little baby."

A phone rang, startling Shannon out of her dream. She glanced at the bedside alarm clock. It was 9:15 p.m. The last thing she remembered was letting herself into her friend's house. She'd been so exhausted she'd kicked off her shoes and lain down on the bed. Evidently she'd fallen asleep.

The phone rang again. Shannon reached for the receiver. "Dr. Yamana's residence."

"Dr. Yamana's car calling."

"Zoe?" Shannon said, still trying to orient herself. The dream had seemed so real that the fact she was lying fully dressed on the bed in Zoe's guest room didn't compute.

"Who else?" her friend asked blithely. "So, you want to tell me the reason for your sudden visit? And don't give me that stuff about needing to get out of the cabin for a few days.''

Her best friend sounded as bossy as ever. ''I thought you had an emergency,'' she replied, stalling.

''I did. It's been taken care of.'' Zoe spoke brusquely. ''I'm on my way home. Now answer my question.''

''It was raining there for weeks. I just needed to get away for a while.''

''I don't believe you.''

Shannon hadn't really expected her to. They'd met their first year in college, when they'd been assigned as roommates in the dorm. Even coming from different backgrounds and having different goals hadn't stopped them from becoming friends. Eleven years later, Dr. Zoe Yamana knew Shannon better than anyone.

''Shannon?''

Shannon recognized the veiled threat in Zoe's voice. The woman was like a bulldog when she wanted information. Shannon decided she'd be able to handle the inevitable questions better if she wasn't lying down.

''Hold on a sec.'' She swung her legs over the side of the bed and sat up.

''Did I wake you?'' Zoe asked. ''It's barely after nine. Are you ill?''

''No, I'm not ill. Is that all you doctors ever think?'' Sitting on the side of the bed, Shannon stared at a watercolor seascape on the wall, trying to get the dream out of her mind. Trying to come up with an explanation her friend would accept. She couldn't tell her about Caleb. Not over the phone.

''Shannon?''

How did you tell your best friend that after three years of living as a recluse you made love with a man you barely knew? And not just any man. A cop. An SDU agent with a dangerous job that would always come first. How did you explain that a stranger touched you in a way even your husband hadn't? Zoe would think she was nuts. She'd surely send her to a psychiatrist. And she'd be justified.

"Shannon!"

"I'm here."

"Good, then please tell me what's going on with you. I know the last three years have been hard, losing Tony, then your miscarriage. But I thought you'd come to terms with the past and were ready to get on with your life."

The compassion in her friend's voice brought tears to Shannon's eyes. Zoe had been such wonderful support, especially when she'd lost her baby. She'd grieved so for Tony that she hadn't even realized she was pregnant until she'd miscarried.

"Are you still having the dreams?"

Shannon caught her breath. How did Zoe always know?

"You are, aren't you?"

"Yes," Shannon answered quietly, remembering in full detail the dream she'd awoken from just minutes ago. "But this last one was different."

"Different? How?"

It was easy to imagine the look on Zoe's face. Her dark brows would be raised, her jade-green eyes wide with interest and concern. Shannon spoke to that concern. "Usually when I wake up there's this terrible sense of loss. But the dream I just had..." She trailed off, not sure she could explain the way it had filled her heart.

"Maybe it means you've finally accepted the past," Zoe said gently.

Maybe it did, Shannon thought.

"I'm just a couple of blocks away, hon. We'll talk more when I get there."

Shannon nodded, then realized Zoe couldn't see her. "Okay." She hung up the phone, then curled up on the bed. Accepting the past meant she had to start looking to the future. An image of Caleb invaded her mind. She tried to shake it off. Her skin tingled, as if he'd just touched her.

"No!" She sprang off the bed and crossed to the sliding glass door that looked out over the bay. She would not think of how he had reawakened her body. She slid open the door and breathed in the cool sea air. She wasn't going to allow one afternoon of love-making to take over her life.

Just because she'd wanted him... Just because she'd enjoyed having his hands caress her body... Just because his mouth had taken her to the stars and back... Well, none of that said they were meant to be together.

Shannon looked out at the night. A wind had blown the fog away. The sky was now clear and filled with stars. She wondered if Caleb was looking at the stars, too.

Desperate to forget, she closed the door with a hard thunk and pulled the drapes.

"Hey! What's that all about?" a voice said from behind her.

Startled, Shannon swung around. "Oh, Zoe. I didn't hear you come in."

Zoe studied her silently until Shannon began to feel like a bug under a microscope.

"Why are you looking at me like that?"

Zoe cocked her head to one side. "You seem… different."

Again Shannon thought, how did she always know?

Zoe walked over, took her by the hand and pulled her out of the room. "I'm starving," she said as they entered the kitchen. "I'm going to fix us something to eat."

The way her emotions were churning, Shannon didn't think she could eat a thing. "I'm fine."

Zoe shook her head. "I don't think so. Now go sit down at the counter and tell me what's going on."

Watching her friend move around the kitchen seemed so comforting and familiar that Shannon knew she couldn't hold back any longer. She took a deep breath. "I've met someone."

Zoe placed two glasses on the counter, then filled them with the wine she'd taken out of the refrigerator. She handed one to Shannon and looked at her searchingly. "A man who made you want to run away?"

Shannon shrugged and took a sip of her wine. The problem with Caleb wasn't that she wanted to run away from him, but that she wanted to run *to* him. Her hand began to shake and she set down her glass.

Zoe touched her arm. "There's more to this than you're saying, isn't there?" She paused a moment, then asked gently, "Did you sleep with him?"

Shannon nodded. Tears filled her eyes.

"Shannon, honey, is it possible you're pregnant?"

"*What?*" Shocked, Shannon stared at her friend. "No, of course not." Or was it?

"But you made love with him?"

Shannon's heart started to race. "Only once." Or twice. Or three times. How many times had they made love? And without any protection.

Zoe gave a short laugh. "It only takes once."

"I know," Shannon said. It only took once to get pregnant by a man who was the worst possible choice for her peace of mind. "God, Zoe, how could I have been so reckless?"

"Shannon, listen to me." Zoe spoke in her serious doctor voice. "I don't want you to panic. But you have to consider the possibility."

Consider the possibility. Shannon got up and began pacing the kitchen with knees that had turned to butter. Her life had just taken a dramatic turn. Even if it turned out she wasn't pregnant, she had a lot of thinking to do. Caleb Carlisle had touched her more than just physically. She'd wanted him to stay. She'd wanted a stranger to love her and want her and need her. She'd wanted another cop in her life. Why? Hadn't she learned her lesson the first time?

"Shannon?"

She looked at Zoe. "What do we do? I'll have to take a test. When can I do that?"

Zoe nodded. "A blood test will show the possibility after seven or eight days."

Eight days. She couldn't go home and wait alone. "Would you mind if I stayed with you till then?"

Zoe moved close and gave her a hug. "I'd mind if you didn't."

Chapter Eight

Pregnant.

Shannon had known in her heart before the test that this would be the result. The question now was, how did she feel about it?

Eight days after she'd made her precipitous trip to Monterey, she was on the road again, headed back to her cabin in the Santa Cruz Mountains. Zoe had tried to get her to stay longer, but the consequences of her actions had hit her with the magnitude of an earthquake. Shannon had decisions to make, and she needed the solitude of her own home to make them.

Looking in the rearview mirror so she could change lanes, Shannon caught sight of the slightly panicked expression on her face. "Miss Know-It-All, my eye. You didn't know enough to stop yourself from going to bed with a stranger. And even worse, you didn't know enough to use protection when you did."

That was a lie. She'd known. She just hadn't done anything about it. She'd been so wrapped up in Caleb and the exquisite feelings he'd awoken in her that she hadn't wanted to let go of him, or those sensations, for even a moment.

She wasn't a fool. She knew how irresponsible her

actions had been. And yet, how could she regret that afternoon of lovemaking when it had given her the one thing she'd always wanted?

"It's still early yet, Shannon. You won't be out of trouble for months," Zoe had reminded her solemnly before she'd left her friend's home.

Shannon knew Zoe was worried about her losing the baby as she had before. But Shannon had no doubt that she'd give birth to Caleb's child. What she had to do now was decide what she was going to do about it.

Her exit just ahead, Shannon put on her blinker and moved over into the right-hand lane. As she took the ramp that would put her on the last leg of her journey, she tried not to wonder how Caleb might react to the news of his impending fatherhood.

Not that she was planning to tell him. At least, not yet, not until it was plain to see. So, really, the speculation was irrelevant.

She barely knew the man. And she certainly wasn't going to take any action until she did. His being a law-enforcement officer didn't qualify him for fatherhood. For all she knew, he was just like Tony, reckless and selfish and destined for an early death.

Tears filled her eyes. She blinked them away. She didn't care what she had to do. She was carrying this baby to term. And if that meant keeping the fact of its existence from its father, then that was what she'd do.

A brief siren sounded. She looked in the rear mirror and saw the flashing red lights of a police car. A glance at her speedometer told her she wasn't speeding, but she pulled over, anyway.

She got her license and registration ready to show

the officer. Watching him walk toward her through her side mirror, she realized he was a sheriff, not a highway patrolman. She rolled down the window.

"Hello, ma'am, are you Shannon Garrett?"

Surprised, she nodded. "Yes, I am."

"We've been looking for you over a week, Ms. Garrett. Are you all right?"

She frowned in confusion. Why would they be looking for her? "Of course I'm all right. What's this about?"

Another sheriff's vehicle pulled up in front of her.

"We're here to take you back to Santa Cruz, ma'am. You're wanted as a possible witness in a criminal investigation."

"I haven't witnessed any crime," Shannon told him, utterly bewildered. "Are you sure you have the right person?"

The other deputy walked up to her Jeep. "We're sure, ma'am. You've been named as the person who can confirm SDU Agent Caleb Carlisle's alibi."

"Caleb? Why does he need an alibi?" This was getting more confusing by the moment. She might not have been thrilled that Caleb was a cop, but she had a hard time believing he was a crooked cop. "There must be a mistake."

"That may be, ma'am," the first deputy said. "All we know is there's been an APB out for your vehicle the past week with orders to bring you in for questioning."

She nodded. "Anything to help clear up the matter." Especially in her own mind. "Can you tell me where I'm supposed to go?"

"One of us will take you, Ms. Garrett."

Typical cop arrogance, she thought, irritated. "I am

not going to leave my Jeep on the side of the road, Deputy. One of you can escort me in if you're worried I won't get there.''

The deputies had a brief discussion, which ended with the decision that one would lead and one would follow.

As the three of them eased back onto the highway, Shannon couldn't stop thinking about the possibility of her child's father committing a crime. Was this one of those be-careful-what-you-wish-for lessons? She'd balked at the idea of a cop fathering her baby, so she'd gotten a criminal, instead?

"YES, MA'AM, I UNDERSTAND." Caleb held the receiver between his shoulder and neck and reached for a citizen-complaint form. "Can you describe the man?"

He dutifully wrote down a description that sounded like every other teenage boy in the U.S. He looked around at the office, full of scarred desks, empty of people. Everyone else was out doing something, except the captain, who was back in his office, probably dreaming up some other boring job for him.

God, he was tired of desk duty. Eight days had passed since he'd been brought in. Knox and Munoz were doing all they could to investigate the Driscoe fiasco, but they weren't a part of the undercover operation as he was.

Every day that went by without solving the murders of the Driscoe brothers only frustrated him more. Larkin was nowhere to be found. As for the mysterious Mick... Damn, he should be out there beating the bushes for the bad guys, instead of in here getting paper cuts!

The insistent voice of his caller demanded his attention. "Yes, ma'am, I'm listening. Yes, I understand. Yes, ma'am, someone will be out to check on it."

Caleb hung up, then rubbed his neck, trying to relieve the tension that had plagued him for days. Shannon was still missing, Brandon was still in a coma, and he was stuck in the office fielding complaints from paranoid old ladies.

"Got a new pile of statistics for you, Carlisle."

Caleb glared up at Sean Gallagher.

The captain smiled sympathetically. "Sorry, pal. Until your alibi's confirmed, this is your job."

"My fingerprints weren't on the murder weapon. Isn't that enough? Or do you think I wiped the prints, too?"

Gallagher rested his hip on the edge of Caleb's desk. "Cool your jets, Carlisle, or I won't share the new information on your case I just received."

The glitter in Captain Gallagher's eyes indicated something good. "What's up? Is it Brandon? Is he out of the coma?"

Gallagher shook his head. "No, I'm sorry, but it does have to do with him. One of the guys found his weapon this morning. We had the lab test it, and something interesting turned up."

Caleb raised a brow and waited for his boss to finish.

"Henry Driscoe was not killed by a bullet from Agent Everly's gun."

Caleb stood. "Are you sure?"

Gallagher nodded.

"So there was someone else out there. Larkin." It had to have been Larkin. If it had been the Driscoes'

Mick, Jim wouldn't have told J.P. to call him. "But why would he kill one of the Driscoes?"

"Maybe he was aiming for you or Brandon," Gallagher suggested.

Caleb shook his head. "He'd have to have been an awfully bad shot. But the other brothers ended up dead, too, so maybe Larkin and this Mick guy planned it all along. Dammit, Captain, you have to let me off desk duty!"

Gallagher pushed off from the desk. "Don't give me grief over this. My hands are tied. And you know the rules."

Caleb scowled. "And you know I didn't shoot those men."

Frustration tightened Gallagher's expression. "The bullets came from your gun, so until you can prove you weren't anywhere near those men when they were killed, you'll just have to stay put."

The door opened behind them, causing them both to swing around. Two sheriff's deputies walked in, followed by the most beautiful sight Caleb had ever seen.

"Shannon."

He looked her over from head to toe, searching for any sign she'd been hurt. She looked different from the way she had the day he'd left her cabin, but he could see she was all right.

He allowed the relief to flood through him as he turned his attention to her face. What he saw surprised him. He'd expected mistrust, dislike, even disgust; after all, she'd been brought in because he'd been accused of a crime. But instead, she seemed to be searching his expression as intensely as he was hers.

He tried to read the questions in her eyes and saw only shadows and secrets.

Captain Gallagher stepped in front of him, offering his hand to Shannon and introducing himself. "I appreciate your coming in, ma'am."

She shook her hand. "I'm not sure what this is all about, Captain, but—"

Gallagher cut her off before she could continue. "Why don't you come into my office and we'll talk," he said, gesturing toward the back.

Shannon gave Caleb another unreadable look, then allowed his captain to escort her into his office. The door closed behind them.

THE CAPTAIN MOTIONED her to the chair in front of his battle-scarred wooden desk, then sat in his own chair, dwarfing the large leather chair with his size. She supposed his intimidating size came in handy for his profession. She hoped very much that this man was on Caleb's side.

Everything she'd needed to know had been broadcast on Caleb's face the moment he saw her. There'd been no fear of exposure in his melted-ice eyes, only worry, followed by relief. Her disappearance had concerned him. If he'd known what she'd learned when she'd left the area, it probably would have concerned him even more.

She shook off the thought. She had no intention of telling Caleb Carlisle about his impending fatherhood at this time.

"I'm sorry we had to bring you in like this, Ms. Garrett. But there are some questions I need to ask you."

She fixed her gaze on his face. "That's all right, Captain. I have a question of my own."

He raised a dark eyebrow. "Oh?"

She nodded. "How on earth could you possibly think a dedicated officer like Caleb Carlisle would need an alibi for anything?"

Captain Gallagher showed no surprise at her question. "I was under the impression that you'd never met Agent Carlisle before he showed up injured at your cabin."

"I hadn't," she confirmed, not bothering to keep the irritation out of her voice.

"Yet you think you know him well enough to say he'd never commit a crime?"

"Are you saying he *has* committed a crime?" she asked. The almost twenty-four hours she'd spent with Caleb had given her a good idea of his priorities. His job was on the top of his list. Otherwise, he wouldn't have left her to go back into a potentially dangerous situation.

Captain Gallagher looked at her searchingly. "Ms. Garrett, did Agent Carlisle tell you what happened to him that brought him injured to your doorstep?"

Because she didn't see how it could harm Caleb, she gave the captain a brief description of what had happened the night she'd found Caleb on her porch. The captain interrupted with questions periodically to clarify a point. The only thing she left out was the intimacy that had developed them. She didn't consider it any of his business.

"So you're saying that Agent Carlisle's partner was his main concern during the time he spent at your cabin?"

"Yes, Captain, that is what I'm saying," Shannon

answered patiently. "It's what I've said several times." She'd been very touched by Caleb's obvious loyalty to and affection for his partner. Tony had always avoided emotional ties with his partners. He thought being friends with fellow officers would put him and them at risk, that they'd be too worried about one another's welfare to do their jobs. She often wondered if that was why he'd kept a certain distance from her, too.

"Ms. Garrett?"

She brought her attention back to the captain. "Yes?"

"Do you think it's possible that Agent Carlisle was so worried about his partner because he was the one who'd caused his injuries?"

Shannon was stunned. "His partner was injured? And you think Caleb did it deliberately?"

"Agent Everly was found unconscious with a bullet wound in his back," Captain Carlisle told her, his expression grave. "The bullet came from Agent Carlisle's gun."

Shannon suspected the captain was trying to shock her into some sort of reaction. It didn't work. "Caleb walked miles, in spite of his own injuries, looking for help, and you think he shot his partner in the back and left him to die?"

"That's not what I said."

No, she thought, but was it what he'd meant? She searched the tough handsome face, but couldn't see beyond the grave expression.

"You said Agent Carlisle was very worried about his partner," he continued. "Why did it take him so long to return to the compound?"

Shannon gripped the arms of the chair, wishing she

could throw the darn thing. "What would you have had him do, Captain?" she asked fiercely. "Swim back? It was pouring rain, the creek at the end of my road was impassable. On top of that, he had a concussion and a sprained ankle. And in spite of all that, he left the minute the weather broke, twenty-four hours after he arrived."

"Let's get back to my original question. Do you believe Agent Carlisle was so worried about his partner because he was the one who'd shot him?"

Did she think the man who'd made tender passionate love to her, the father of her unborn child, was a cold-blooded killer?

"Ms. Garrett?"

She looked Captain Gallagher dead in the eye. "Absolutely not."

The phone rang, shattering the silence left after her declaration. The captain answered, grunted monosyllabic replies a couple of times, then hung up.

He rose from his chair. "I'm going to ask Agent Carlisle to join us." He opened the door and left the office.

Moments later he was back, followed by Caleb.

"Sit down, Carlisle," the captain ordered.

Caleb took the chair next to Shannon's, but kept his gaze on his superior. It gave her a chance to study his appearance. More than a week had passed since he'd left in Harvey Moran's PG&E truck. The lump on his forehead had gone down, his bruises had faded some, but healing hadn't brought peace of mind, she sensed.

Caleb wore jeans and a light-blue button-down shirt. The collar was left open, and the sleeves were rolled up just below his elbows. The muscles of his exposed forearms seemed bunched and tense. His big hands gripped the arms of his chair, as hers had done earlier. Frustration radiated from him. He reminded her of a caged panther. Though he sat absolutely still, she suspected he was pacing inside.

"What's going on, Captain?" he asked.

The deepness of his voice sparked her blood. She'd forgotten the timbre of it, like rich velvet.

"Well, Caleb, you seem to have found an ally in Ms. Garrett. According to her statement, you arrived at her cabin at 7 p.m. The autopsy report for both Driscoe brothers states that they died instantly between the hours of 7 and 9 p.m. Since you were three miles away at the time, this pretty much clears you of those murders."

Relief filled her. She was afraid the captain hadn't believed her.

"Does that mean I'm back on the case?"

At Caleb's question, Shannon's relief was replaced by dread. The man had been accused of murder by his own agency, yet he was raring to get back to work?

"No, Agent Carlisle, it doesn't. We still don't know who shot Agent Everly with your weapon."

"It wasn't me," Caleb gritted out. "The fact that I'm clear for the Driscoes' deaths should tell you that someone else had access to my gun."

Captain Gallagher shrugged. "Nevertheless, you are too close to the situation to be an effective investigator."

Caleb jumped to his feet. "Someone tried to set me up, and you expect me to sit here shuffling paper while this person leaves the country for who knows

where? Brandon and I have been working on this for
months. You have to let me finish the job!''

And end up with a bullet in *your* back? Shannon
bit her lip to keep herself from saying the words
aloud. If Caleb was allowed to investigate this strange
situation, he could be the one to get shot this time.

Well, she had no intention of sticking around to
see that happen. Enough was enough. Both men
watched as she stood, her purse clutched in both
hands. Shannon ignored the spark in Caleb's eyes and
looked, instead, at his boss. ''If you don't have any
more questions, Captain, I'm leaving.''

''I'm going to need you to sign your statement
once it gets typed up. I should have it for you in an
hour.''

She nodded. ''I'll be back then.''

Caleb could hardly believe the chill in her voice.
What had happened to the warm woman who had
cared for his wounds and touched his body with such
passion? ''Shannon, wait.''

She stopped in the open doorway but didn't turn
around.

He walked over to her and placed a hand on her
arm. Electricity leaped between them. It might have
been the nylon carpet under their feet that caused it,
but the carpet had nothing to do with how glad he
was to see her again. ''I need to talk to you,'' he said
quietly. ''Can you wait in the office while I finish
here?''

She looked at him, her eyes shadowed. ''I don't
have much time. I have something I have to do.''

There was an odd undercurrent in her voice. ''It's
important, Shannon.''

Her gaze indicated reluctance and something else. "I really don't think it's a good idea."

He couldn't blame her after the way he'd left, but his gut told him not to let her go off on her own. "Please wait for me."

She stared at him for a moment, then agreed. He walked her over to his desk, then went back to the captain's office.

Shannon sat at Caleb's desk as she'd been asked and wondered why she was there. She hadn't fought the idea of talking to him at all. It was nuts! She'd acted like some docile house pet. At this rate she'd be spilling the beans about the baby in no time.

She shifted in her seat, staring at the closed door of Captain Gallagher's office. The very thought of sharing her news with a man who carried a gun for a living was intolerable. The man who was in that very office, trying to talk his boss into putting him back on the streets to investigate criminals who'd set him up. If they'd gone to so much trouble in the first place, surely they wouldn't hesitate to shoot him the moment he got close enough.

The door to the outside opened, drawing her attention. Two men walked in. There was no doubt in Shannon's mind that the duo were fellow agents of Caleb's. The swagger in the walk. The observant gaze, recording every detail,.

One was a muscular Hispanic man of medium height, with dark soulful eyes and a handsome face. He appeared to be in his early thirties.

The other man was older, late forties at least, tall, with graying blond hair. He had the cynical look of a veteran cop. Shannon had seen that world-weary expression many times on the faces of Tony's superior officers.

The two men nodded as they passed her, then went straight to the captain's office. The older man knocked twice, then opened the door and went in. The other man followed.

INSIDE GALLAGHER'S OFFICE, Caleb stared at Malcolm Knox. "What do you mean this investigation has put Shannon in danger? I was at her house less than twenty-four hours. She bandaged me up and sent me on my way. Why would Larkin and this Mick guy care one way or another?"

"It's possible they don't," Knox said. "But I'm not sure we should take the chance."

The idea of Shannon being brought into this ugly situation because he'd just happened to choose her porch to collapse on gnawed at Caleb's insides.

He looked at the other agents. "The evidence they left behind to implicate me in the murders has delayed the investigation long enough to allow them to cover their tracks. Our men might have confiscated the drugs, but *they* have the money. What else could they want?"

"You," Sid Munoz replied. "Knox is right. How can they be sure the Driscoes didn't say something, give you some clue that would reveal Mick's identity?"

"And if they had, who's to say you didn't drop some info during the twenty-fours you spent at Ms. Garrett's cabin?" the captain added.

Knox nodded his agreement. "Anything you might have let slip makes Ms. Garrett a target."

Caleb jumped up, furious. "That's ridiculous! I

would never put a civilian in danger. You know me better than that.''

''We're the good guys,'' Knox said calmly. ''How well do the bad guys know you?''

''Not as well as they're going to once I get a hold of them,'' Caleb snarled.

''In the meantime,'' Sid interjected reasonably, ''we need to decide what we're going to do about it. So why don't you sit down and relax?''

Caleb sat, but nothing could make him relax until he knew for sure that Shannon's life was not in danger.

ALONE IN THE OUTSIDE OFFICE, Shannon wondered why she was still sitting there when all she had to do was get up and leave. She stood and looked around, thinking she would do just that, when a framed photo on the wall caught her attention.

She walked over to it. It looked as if it had been taken at some company get-together. Caleb's smiling face was the first she noticed. Flashing his dimple, he looked happy and cocky and totally full of himself. The captain was there, also smiling, as were the two men who'd just walked in.

She turned her attention to the remaining figure in the photograph. He was taller than the other four, and whipcord lean, an arresting figure. His dark-blond hair was wavy and a little long. He probably had a hard time keeping it out of his sky-blue eyes.

As her gaze returned to Caleb, she compared the two and decided they were like night and day.

''The one in the yellow shirt is Brandon Everly, my partner.''

Shannon started at the sound of Caleb's voice. She

glanced at him, then back at the face of his friend. This Brandon seemed so full of life. Maybe it was the grin, she thought. With a grin like that, he was sure to have the ladies falling at his feet. It was hard to imagine him lying in a hospital bed, felled by a bullet.

She looked back at Caleb. "Will he be okay?"

He shrugged, but there was nothing casual about it. "He's in a coma. The doctors can't be sure of anything until he wakes up."

She touched his arm. "I'm sorry."

He gazed down at her. Her eyes met his, saw the barely banked flames of desire and felt her breath catch at the intensity of her body's reaction to that heat.

"Come home with me, Shannon."

She shook her head. "I can't."

He grasped her hands. "You can. We have things to talk about. I have things to tell you. There's no privacy here."

She thought of pulling her hands from his, but found she had no desire to end the connection. "I really don't think that's a good idea. Maybe we could go have a cup of coffee somewhere." It flashed into her mind that caffeine wasn't good for pregnant women. Shannon swung away from him, fearful he might read her secret in her eyes.

Caleb put his hands on her shoulders and leaned close to her ear. "I don't want coffee."

I want you.

The words remained unspoken, but Shannon didn't need to hear them. She knew. "Caleb, I can't…we can't…" She turned around, intent on convincing him that the two of them together would never work. But the minute she looked into his eyes, she couldn't remember even one of the hundred reasons she'd come up with.

"Come home with me, Shannon."

It was both a plea and a command. And simply irresistible. In her eyes he was no longer a cop. He was the man who'd made love to her. The man who was the father of the tiny being she carried beneath her heart. How could she just walk away from him? Didn't she owe it to their child to at least give him a chance?

"Shannon?"

She focused on Caleb's unsmiling face. He put out his hand. Fatalistically Shannon lay her hand in his. His fingers closed over hers.

"You won't be sorry."

No, thought Shannon, *I probably will be.* Nevertheless she allowed the father of her child to lead her from the precinct and out into the fading daylight.

"We'll take your Jeep, if you don't mind," Caleb said as they crossed the parking lot.

Shannon thought fast. She'd counted on having time to rehearse what she had to say to him. How was she supposed to think with him sitting next to her? "Why take only one car?" she asked, trying to sound as if she didn't care one way or another.

"It'll be easier that way." He reached out and took the keys from her stiff fingers. "The directions to my place are kind of complicated, especially this time of day when the traffic starts getting congested."

She could handle the traffic, Shannon thought. The way her life had been turned upside down, traffic was the least of her problems. "But if you leave your car here, you'll have no transportation."

"No problem," he told her as he unlocked the driver's door. "I've got my bike."

He held open the door and she got in. Seconds later he joined her. His closeness, his warmth, his scent, enveloped her. Her brain had simply stepped aside, allowing her senses to take over.

"Turn right at the next corner."

Tempted to turn the car around and head back the way they'd come, Shannon stifled the impulse and followed Caleb's directions.

He kept his arm draped casually on the back of her seat. And though he didn't touch her, her skin tingled with the memory of how his big hands had caressed every inch of her body. Darn it, she wished she hadn't remembered that!

He didn't talk much, but every time his deep quiet voice broke the silence to give directions, it set butterflies flitting around her stomach. And his scent—warm, spicy, down-to-earth. God, she thought, no man should smell so good.

Shannon braked for the stop sign Caleb had mentioned and waited for more directions. When he didn't say anything, she glanced at him. He was staring at the side mirror, a frown on his face.

"What's wrong?"

He looked over at her. "I think we're being followed."

The butterflies in her stomach turned to bees. "Followed by whom?" She looked in the rear mirror, trying to see which car had made Caleb suspicious. She'd lost the two-toned sedan more than a week ago. Surely it hadn't happened upon her the moment she got back to town, had it?

He looked in the mirror again. "I don't know. It

could be someone the captain sent to keep an eye on me.''

''Why would he do that? I thought my statement cleared you.''

He shrugged. ''I'm not sure anything will clear me until they catch the real culprit.''

In spite of the fact she'd wanted to get away from him, that bothered her. Why would they use precious manpower to follow Caleb when they should be looking for the bad guys? The answer that came into her mind was that they wouldn't, which brought her back to the two-toned sedan.

''Turn left here, Shannon. My condo complex is two blocks ahead on the right.''

She didn't move. Going to his place didn't make sense to her. ''But what if they're still following us?''

Again he shrugged. ''If it's someone from the agency, then they already know where I live.''

''And if it's not?''

''We'll cross that bridge if we come to it,'' he said.

The touch of grit in his voice reminded her, unnecessarily, that this was a man of the law. She looked over at him. Lord, the man was a feast for the eyes. Big, strong, all male. Dark and yet somehow comforting. Like the way she felt on a winter night when she lay in her big brass bed, covered warmly in layers of quilts.

Don't, Shannon. She mentally shook herself as she once again followed his directions. It had been all too easy to fall under Caleb's spell when he'd been injured and under her care. But she had to be practical. It wasn't just *her* happiness at stake now, but the happiness of their baby.

The man was an undercover drug agent who'd just

been framed for the attempted murder of his partner. The distraction of an unplanned pregnancy was the last thing he needed right now. But he did need to know that the person who tailed them just might be the same person who'd followed her to Monterey last week.

''Caleb, there's something you should know.''

Chapter Nine

"Let me get this straight," Caleb said through what she suspected were gritted teeth. "Some jerk followed you all the way from Santa Cruz to Monterey and you didn't call the police?"

"That's right," she answered patiently, in spite of the fact he was speaking to her as if she was an idiot.

"Turn in the first driveway."

She did as he directed.

"You can park in my space. Third on the left."

She pulled into the space he'd pointed out, narrowly missing the enormous black motorcycle parked between her bumper and the wall. She turned off the engine.

"I've got my bike," she recalled him saying. She thought he'd meant a bicycle, a common sight in health-conscious Santa Cruz. Silly girl, she scolded herself. How much more proof did she need that this man was just as reckless as the one who'd made her a widow at twenty-six?

Caleb turned to her. "So why didn't you call the police?"

She took the key out of the ignition. "What was I supposed to tell them, Caleb? That I'd been followed by a two-toned car whose color I couldn't distinguish and whose license plate I never saw? They would have written my complaint off as paranoia and you know it.''

Without answering, Caleb walked around to open her door. Avoiding his outstretched hand, she got out and locked the door. She couldn't stand the thought of him touching her right now. Her nerves felt as taut as guitar strings, and her emotions were too close to the surface. She wanted to fling herself into his arms; she wanted to run as far and fast from him as she could.

They walked side by side across the parking lot.

''All you had to do was tell the police who you were,'' Caleb said finally. 'They wouldn't have written off a well-known newspaper columnist. Trying to lose that guy on your own was very reckless.''

Shannon stuck her hands into the pockets of her jeans. It was the only way she could control fingers that ached to touch him. Although whether she wanted to strangle him or caress him she wasn't sure. Who was he to call *her* reckless?

''I didn't *try* to lose him, Caleb. I *did* lose him,'' she said haughtily. ''Now can we talk about something else?''

Damning the electricity that buzzed between them, she followed Caleb to the large condominium complex. Painted a weathered-looking gray with white trim, it looked as if it had been transplanted from the sea-swept rocky New England coast.

Arriving at the white wooden steps that led to his front door on the second floor, Caleb stood aside and allowed her to precede him. She walked quickly up the stairs, feeling as if he watched her every move and trying to deny the thrill that went through her.

Waiting for him to open the door, she used the time to silently rehearse the speech she planned to deliver. "Caleb, I won't deny the sexual attraction I feel for you, but we're both mature enough to know it takes more than sex to make a good relationship."

But what we had between us was more than sex, a little voice taunted. She recognized that voice immediately. It was the voice of her impractical, impulsive, romantic side. The side she'd vowed never to let make her life decisions again.

Caleb pushed the door open and gestured her inside.

Like a lamb to the slaughter, she went in and stopped short.

He bumped into her from behind and grasped her arms to steady both of them. "What's the matter?"

She stepped away from him. "Nothing's the matter. Nothing at all."

The truth was undeniable. The place was wonderful. She didn't know what she'd expected. Something more macho-bachelor? But there was nothing macho-bachelor about the large room before her.

The living room and kitchen were connected, separated only by a butcher-block counter. Both areas were decorated in shades of off-white and beige. Coffee table, end tables and dining set were fashioned out of warm-honey pine, as was the wood floor. Houseplants thrived on every surface. A long dark-tan leather sofa faced a wall of French doors. In the distance she could see the ocean.

The combination of earth tones, the fresh green of nature and pale blue of sea and sky lent a serenity to the room that instantly calmed Shannon's nerves. So Caleb wasn't always reckless. This wasn't the apartment of a man who came home to sleep and shower. Caleb had made this a *home*. She instantly tamped down the unbidden thought. It only took one moment of recklessness to end a life.

Or conceive a child.

She swung around to face him. He was much too close. Her body reacted with now-familiar longing. She had to get him away from her. "Could I have a glass of water, please?"

He looked at her strangely. "Sure."

His limp seemed a little more pronounced as he walked into the kitchen. Probably from walking up the stairs too fast, trying to keep up with her, she thought a little guiltily.

Impatient with the trend of her thoughts, she shifted her gaze away from him and crossed to the window. If she went soft on him now, she'd never have a chance. Damn this brain of hers! Her teachers had always told her she thought too much. She'd chosen a profession that demanded she think and research and study and analyze all the time. So why had her mind suddenly turned to mush?

"Here's your water."

Startled, Shannon swung around. Her hand inadvertently knocked the glass from his hand. It fell, spilling its contents on the woven rug beneath their feet but not breaking.

"Oh! I'm sorry!" Shannon moved to pick it up.

Caleb grabbed her arm. "It doesn't matter."

His touch brought desire screaming to the surface. The blood heated in her veins. She gazed up at him and saw her feelings reflected in the blue flame of his eyes. "Caleb."

He pulled her against him and crushed her lips with his own. She clung to him, drinking fully of his mouth, slaking her thirst. She ran her hands over his chest, his shoulders. She tangled her fingers in his thick silky hair and tugged him closer, plunging her tongue into his mouth, tasting him as he had her.

"I want you, Caleb. I want you so much." She'd never wanted anything so much in her life. She wanted to touch every inch of him. She wanted to crawl inside him, to see everything, to know all there was to know.

"I can't stand the thought of that man following you. What if he'd run you into a ditch? What if he'd hurt you?" His hands roamed over her, caressing her breasts, her waist, her hips.

"He didn't," she whispered. "I'm fine." The nerves on the surface of her skin buzzed with anticipation.

"Take it off," she whispered, grazing his neck with her teeth as his hands went under her sweater.

He pushed it up and off in one swift movement, then tossed it onto a nearby wicker chair. She reached for his shirt and started unfastening the small white buttons. Her fingers fumbled in her haste, making her impatient. He solved the problem by grasping the hem and pulling it off over his head.

Instantly they were back in each other's arms, kissing and touching, touching and kissing. Shannon felt as if she could go on forever and never have enough. Her head felt light, as if she was high in the mountains. Her hands felt restless, needing to caress every surface of his hard hair-roughened body.

His nimble fingers released the front clasp of her bra, then stayed to play with her sensitive nipples. Bending his head, he replaced his fingers with his teeth and tongue, licking, sucking, gently scraping. She gasped as an arrow of fire shot down to her most feminine parts. She grabbed his head, forcing his face up, and brought his lips back to her own, opening his mouth, devouring him and begging to be devoured in return.

Suddenly she was floating as Caleb picked her up and carried her into the bedroom, never releasing her lips. He laid her gently on his huge bed and lay down beside her. His big hands cradled her face as he gazed into her eyes. "You're so beautiful. I want you so much." His voice was so full of emotion it brought tears to her eyes.

Gently he kissed them away. Then he kissed her forehead, her cheeks, her mouth, again and again. Shannon could do nothing but want more. Her hands, her mouth, her very being, couldn't seem to get enough of him. "I need you inside me," she gasped.

Pausing only to remove her jeans and his own, Caleb did as she asked. Entering her with exquisite tenderness, he filled her, starting a fire she felt would never be extinguished.

She moved against him, wrapping her legs around his hips. "Take me, Caleb. Take me now."

"Yes," he whispered against her neck. "Yes."

And he plunged into her again and again, driving the flames of her desire higher and higher, until she thought she couldn't handle any more heat, any more ecstasy. But when he gave her more, she took it greedily, happily, ecstatically. And gave everything she had in return.

Unwilling to break the connection, Caleb rolled to his side, pulling Shannon with him. He held her against the length of his body and ran his hand down the long line of her back. He'd never felt skin so soft or been made love to so intensely.

Which made what he had to tell her that much harder.

He glanced at the clock on the bedside table. Thank God he'd told Sid he needed some time. He and Shannon had an hour together before he had to send her away.

"I like your place." Shannon's breath tickled the hairs on his chest. God, she thought, how idiotic! There were a dozen things needing to be said. Decor wasn't even on the list.

Caleb smiled. "What did you expect? A swinging bachelor pad? Velour sofa? Shag rugs? Remote-control light dimmer? Champagne chilling in the fridge?"

Shannon laughed. "I don't think my mind would have gone that far."

"Too bad," he said. "The champagne is the one thing I do have."

Her green eyes sparkled. "A bachelor has to be ready for seduction."

"Well, this bachelor had to come up with a hostess gift for a Christmas party I was invited to and, it turned out, was unable to attend." Just as he'd been walking out the door, his cell phone had rung. An informant who'd given him a tip that the Driscoes had a possible connection in the SDU. *Merry Christmas, let me ruin your holiday.*

"Caleb? Where did you go just now?"

He met Shannon's questioning gaze. "Nowhere

important, just an incident from the past.'' Reminding him how short their time together was. Time he didn't intend to spend thinking about the job he had to do as soon as he secured Shannon's safety.

A shadow crossed Shannon's features. Caleb could have kicked himself. How many times had her husband brushed her off when he was thinking about some case? He didn't want to be tarred with the same brush, but he wasn't ready to tell her his initial reason for bringing her back to his place. Not when she was lying naked in his arms.

Searching for a way to bring the light back to her eyes, he seized upon the conversation they'd had about his condo. ''So now that you know I'm not a swinging bachelor, do you feel a little safer with me?''

Shannon laughed.

The sound of it sent a shaft of pure joy through his body.

''What a question, after what we just did.''

Caleb shifted so he could look down at her smiling face. ''Maybe we should have talked some, gotten to know each other a little more before we made love again.'' He paused to run the fingers of his right hand through her tawny hair. ''But whenever I'm near you I can't seem to keep my hands, and various other body parts, off you. Even now I want to make love to you.''

Her smile vanished and her gaze intensified. ''So, what are you waiting for?''

''Nothing,'' he said, lowering his mouth to hers. ''Nothing at all.''

HALF AN HOUR LATER, Shannon stared at her image in his bathroom mirror, hardly recognizing herself.

Her hair was tousled, her lips swollen from his kisses, and her eyes glowed. She looked relaxed and happy— exactly what she felt, in spite of her anxiety about the baby.

While Caleb had been making love to her, she'd put her secret to the back of her mind. All he had to do was look at her, and her skin heated from longing for his touch. That she could feel this way about a virtual stranger still amazed her. That she felt this way about an officer of the law scared her to death.

Her purse lay on the counter. She took out her brush and started untangling her hair. How was she supposed to reconcile her fear with her need? How was she supposed to tell a man she couldn't get enough of that their relationship would have to entail a lot more than great sex? She knew nothing about the man. She had no idea how he'd react to the news. She couldn't expect him to be happy about it. At least, not right away.

Maybe not ever.

Oh, God, what had she done? The brush fell from her nerveless fingers, clattering on the counter. How could she have become more deeply involved with Caleb when she was keeping such an important secret?

There was a knock on the door. "Shannon, are you okay?"

She took a deep breath before answering. "I'm fine, Caleb."

"I have your clothes."

She went to the door and opened it a few inches.

Dressed in jeans and a blue T-shirt, Caleb smiled. "Are you sure you want to put these on?"

A bolt of desire went through her, and she realized she'd quite willingly go back to his bed. She held out her hand. "I think I'd better." It would be much easier to handle her feelings for him clothed and with some distance between them.

"Oh, all right." With an exaggerated sigh of reluctance, he handed them to her. "I'll go make us something to eat."

"Good idea," she said brightly, and shut the door.

Maybe food would get her mind working properly again, she thought as she dressed. There had to be a solution to the mess she'd gotten herself into.

Immediately she regretted the thought. She spread her hand over her still-flat stomach. *I'm sorry, baby,* she said silently, *you aren't the mess. You're a miracle. And I'm going to do my best to give you the life you deserve.*

But didn't that mean a mother and a father? the little voice inside her asked.

She looked at her reflection, read the doubt in her expression. She wanted to say no. A child could be happy with one parent, couldn't he? But past experience reared its head. Hadn't she put off having a child with Tony because she was afraid he wasn't going to be around to help raise their child?

You can't have it both ways, Shannon.

CALEB CALLED SID. "Find out if Larkin owns a two-toned sedan. Shannon was followed the night she left her cabin. It might have been a coincidence, but I don't think so."

Having bought them an extra hour together, he then went to the kitchen to make some sandwiches. It wasn't a long drive to Moss Landing, but he needed some excuse to keep her with him just a little longer. Now all he had to do was convince her to go along with the plan.

But first he had to take care of her, he thought now as he cut the sandwiches into halves. Lunch first, then a long frank talk. Shannon was an intelligent woman. She'd understand why she had to be put somewhere safe for a few days.

A moment later Shannon walked out of the bedroom and joined him in the kitchen. "Whoa, I hope you're not expecting me to eat all those sandwiches. I'm not *that* hungry."

Following the focus of her vision, Caleb looked down at the counter. Six sandwiches were lined up on the butcher-block surface. Six! He'd been so preoccupied he hadn't realized what he'd been doing. "Oops."

Shannon laughed. "Oops? What were you thinking?"

He walked around the counter and took her in his arms. "I was thinking about you." It was only a half lie, but he regretted having to do it all the same.

He kissed her briefly on the lips. "Why don't you go sit at the table by the window? I'll bring lunch over."

She looked to see where he'd gestured—a round, glass-topped table flanked by two wicker chairs. Then she smiled. "Just one sandwich for me, okay?"

He watched her walk to the table. Her long mint-green sweater hugged her hips over the snug jeans. The gentle sway as she moved made him wish he could take her back to bed.

She took a seat on one of the chairs and gazed out the window. "This is a wonderful view."

Caleb picked up the two plates he'd arranged and brought them over. "I was lucky to get this unit."

She cocked her head. "Why do I think there's a story behind that statement?"

"Nothing all that exciting, I'm afraid." He went back to the refrigerator to retrieve the two glasses of milk he'd poured earlier, then returned to the table. "It just turned out I'd met the previous owner years before when I was a rookie cop."

She nodded, not taking her eyes off his face. "And?"

He shrugged. "And he felt some gratitude toward me."

"Because?"

Caleb picked up a sandwich half. "Been practicing your interrogation techniques?"

"How else do you think I acquire all that information I put in my columns? You're stalling, Caleb." She took a swallow of her milk, then set the glass down. "Was it a bribe?"

"No, it wasn't a bribe," he snapped, insulted. "I saved the guy's life, okay?"

She grinned. "Okay."

He shook his head, disgusted with himself. "I should have known better than to mess with an intelligent woman."

"Yes, you should have," she said, and took a bite of her sandwich. "Mmm, this is great. Did you grow up in Santa Cruz?"

"Nope, San José," he said, gobbling the other half of his sandwich.

All the better not to have to answer questions? she thought as she watched him chew. That was all right. She was patient. She waited until he'd taken a swallow of milk, then continued, "I'm from San José, too. We might have grown up blocks from each other and never known."

"I doubt that," he said with a wry smile.

She raised a brow. "Why do you say that?"

He looked at her, his blue eyes sharp. She could almost feel him gauging how much to tell her. "If you'd hung around my neighborhod, you'd have been eaten alive."

"That bad, huh?"

"Worse."

The brief statement spoke volumes. "You obviously made it out. How did you end up as a drug-enforcement agent?"

"You really want the story of my life?"

Shannon nodded. She wanted it. Even more important, their baby deserved it. Caleb had a dangerous job. If something bad happened to him one day, she wanted to be able to tell their child about his father.

Caleb sketched out in stark detail a childhood no one deserved. Just months after the birth of his sister, his father had deserted the family. Caleb had been seven. His mother had worked hard to clothe and feed him and his sister, but she hadn't been a very loving mother. By the time he was eleven, he'd started hanging out with the wrong people. He'd committed some petty crime—shoplifting, picking pockets—but by the grace of God hadn't been caught.

"When I was twelve, my mother ran off with a guy she'd been seeing," he continued. "The authorities put me and my sister into foster care."

He kept his voice void of emotion, but Shannon's heart broke for the two children. "I'm so sorry, Caleb."

He shrugged. "I survived. But not before getting myself into more trouble. I owed some money to a friend and had no way to pay him. My foster parents would have been furious if I'd asked them for money. So when he gave me a couple of joints to sell, I felt I didn't have a choice." He smiled wryly. "Luckily I tried to sell them to an undercover cop. I was fifteen."

"Oh, you poor kid! Did he arrest you?"

Caleb shook his head. "No, he took me under his wing, got me involved in a youth-at-risk program and turned me around. It was the best thing that could have happened to me."

"So that's why you joined the SDU." Shannon had never liked the idea of getting involved with another cop, but how could she resent his job when she realized the path his life *could* have taken?

"That's why," Caleb said. "And that's why I have to go after the men who shot Brandon."

Shannon stared at him. "What? I thought you were taken off the case."

He shrugged. "I've put myself back on it. These men target high schools to sell their drugs. The sooner they're put behind bars, the better chance some other kids will survive their childhood. I owe it to them— and to my partner."

Shannon saw red. The red of blood when these men who'd shot his partner turned their weapons on Caleb. The red of anger at the thought of losing another man to cruel violence. "And what about your own child? What do you owe him?"

Chapter Ten

Caleb was confused. "What child? I don't have a child."

Shannon's eyes snapped with fire. She crossed her arms and said nothing. She didn't have to.

His heart started to pound. "You're pregnant."

She nodded.

Joy and fear assailed him at once. He'd always liked children. Even as a kid, he'd sworn when he had some of his own, he'd do right by them. He'd never abandon them the way his parents had him and his sister. But he knew there were those in the world who saw children as pawns. If Knox was right and Mick and Larkin were coming after him, then it was even more imperative that he put Shannon somewhere safe.

"Aren't you going to say anything?"

Caleb reached for her hand. Her voice had a hard edge to it, but he heard an undercurrent of vulnerability that was echoed in the deep shadows of her eyes.

She pushed back her chair and walked several feet away from the table. She hugged herself, then rubbed her arms as if she were cold.

Caleb stood and faced her. "Shannon—"

She didn't let him finish. "I want to know what you're going to do."

What was he going to do? There was no doubt in his mind. He took a couple of steps toward her. "I'm going to be the best father that child can have."

"So you're planning on being there for him or her?"

Her tone was so chilly it made him shiver. Did she doubt his integrity so much? "Of course I'm going to be there."

"Alive?"

So *that* was where this was going. In spite of her forbidding stance, he closed the space between them and put his arms around her. "Of course alive."

He felt her body tremble in reaction to his words, but she kept her face averted. Tenderness coursed through him. He tilted her chin up so he could look her in the eye. "I'm not Tony, honey. I'll never act recklessly on the job."

She pushed him away. "How naive do you think I am?" she asked bitterly. "How stupid?"

"I don't think you're stupid at all," he told her, starting to feel a little angry himself. "I understand this isn't an easy situation for you, but you're going to have to try to trust me."

"Trust you? I don't know you. You don't know me. In nine months we're going to have a baby, and we don't know anything about each other—except this!" In two strides she closed the gap between them. Less than a second later she was pulling his head down and crushing his mouth with hers.

Caleb immediately felt the heat in his body begin to build. His mouth reacted to the unspoken demands and demanded of her in return. The kiss was hot and wet and passionate and went on and on.

And then it was over.

They stood staring at each other, panting, speechless.

Caleb swallowed and tried to talk, but found he had no voice. He couldn't find the words to tell her how she'd filled his heart, that he hadn't stopped thinking of her for one moment during the past week. He wanted to tell her he loved her, but he didn't think he could say the words out loud.

He'd only said them to one person in his life—the little sister who'd been taken from him.

He didn't want Shannon taken from him. He wanted her in his life forever. The baby, too.

"I want you to stay away from those men," she said.

"What?" The words were so different from what he expected to hear from her, he doubted his own ears.

"I want you to stay away from those men," she repeated.

He looked at her, focused on her face. Her cheeks were flushed and her eyes were bright with tears she refused to let fall. He saw pride in her expression and a lot of determination. Or was that stubbornness? Maybe enough to match his own. What did that mean for their future?

It didn't matter at the moment. It couldn't. It might be a cliché, but a man *did* have to do what a man had to do. "You're right, Shannon," he said quietly. "We don't know each other. If we did, you wouldn't ask me to leave this job unfinished."

"Even if finishing it might finish you?"

Caleb had hoped to be able to ease into this, but circumstances were changing too rapidly. "It's not me I'm worried about being in danger. It's you."

Her eyes widened.

"I'm sorry I had to tell you so bluntly, but I have reason to believe that the men I'm after might use you against me."

She turned without speaking and walked back to the table, where she sat in one of the wicker chairs. She took a sip of milk from her glass. Then she looked at him. "You'd never met me until you showed up at my cabin a week ago. Why would they think I had enough importance to you to matter?"

Because you do, Caleb thought. From nearly the first moment he'd seen her, she'd achieved an importance in his life he could neither explain nor deny. But to say that to her now would smack more of manipulation than sincerity, he suspected.

Instead, he said, "Don't you think it's more than a coincidence that some guy followed you for miles on the very day I left your cabin?"

She frowned. "That was just some looney who needed driving lessons."

"Maybe," he said, "and maybe not. Do you want to take that chance? Criminals like Larkin and this Mick character don't have enough sensitivity to think about a personal relationship. They just want a way to save their own skin.

"You're the only witness who can prove I was not out there shooting my partner and the Driscoes," he explained. "As long as I was the key suspect, they were safe—at least in their eyes."

"Why wouldn't they just leave the area, or the country, for that matter?" she asked.

It was a good question. "There could be a lot of reasons they haven't left. They know we have people on the lookout for them. They could have been injured, before they killed the Driscoes and shot Brandon." They could be out for revenge, he thought. And what better way than to harm the woman who saved his life?

The phone rang. He crossed to the kitchen counter and picked it up. "Carlisle."

"Everly's awake." It was the captain. "He's asking for you. Won't talk to anyone else."

"I'll be right there," Caleb said, and hung up.

"Who was that?" Shannon asked from behind him. He turned. "The captain. Brandon's awake."

"So let's go." Grabbing the purse she'd set on the counter, she moved toward the door.

Caleb stayed where he was. "You're not going anywhere."

She shrugged. "I'm not staying here."

"I have a friend coming to take you somewhere safe."

She crossed her arms in a stubborn way that was becoming more and more familiar. "When?"

He looked his watch. Damn! Knox and Munoz wouldn't be there for another thirty minutes.

"Are you sure you want to wait that long to talk to your partner?" Shannon asked.

He glared at her. "Are you reading my mind?"

"They don't call me Miss Know-It-All for nothing." Her smile was slight.

Caleb didn't waste time arguing, which relieved Shannon greatly. In spite of her smug pronouncement, she had no idea what was going to happen, and there were things they needed to talk about, now that she'd gone against her better judgment and told him about her pregnancy. The ride to the hospital would give them that opportunity.

They walked down to the Jeep, which Caleb insisted on driving.

Shannon had decided to wait until they were on their way to discuss the future. But one look at Caleb's grim expression as he drove made it clear this was not the time. The discussion would have to wait.

Captain Gallagher was pacing the hospital corridor when they arrived. "It's about time you got here."

Caleb searched the captain's face. "How is he?"

"Come see for yourself," the other man said gruffly, then took off down the long corridor.

Captain Gallagher had always taken it personally when one of his men got hurt.

Keeping Shannon close by his side, Caleb followed the captain to the intensive-care unit.

An officer was posted outside Brandon's room.

"This is Agent Carlisle," Captain Gallagher told him. "He's the only one allowed into this room besides me, understand?"

The officer nodded. "Yes, Captain."

"Brandon says he'll only talk to you," the captain said, looking not at all happy about the situation. "I'll wait with Ms. Garrett in that room." He pointed to a door marked Conference Room. "Come in as soon as you're done."

It was Caleb's turn to nod. He squeezed Shannon's hand, then entered Brandon's room.

His friend and partner lay on a bed barely long enough for his tall body. The only noise in the room was the normal buzz and beep of the monitors. This wasn't the first time he'd seen Brandon since he'd been shot, though it was the first time he'd been allowed to see him alone. But Caleb still had a hard time getting used to his usually loquacious partner lying silent and unmoving.

He crossed to the side of the bed. "Brandon?"

His partner opened his eyes. "Caleb?"

Caleb smiled in relief. Over the past few days he'd begun to wonder if he'd ever be able to talk to his friend again. "It's me, buddy. How ya doin'?"

"I'm okay."

The slight slur in his voice said differently, Caleb thought. "You will be."

"Thought the slide got you."

The memory of tons of rock headed straight for him made Caleb shudder. "It tried."

Brandon tried to smile, then seemed to doze off.

Caleb looked at the monitors, but every little beep seemed the same.

Suddenly Brandon grabbed his arm. "Caleb…have to tell you…can't trust…" He scowled. "Can't…"

Caleb gripped his friend's hand. "Calm down. Everything's going to be fine."

"No!" Brandon almost yelled. "The money…"

"The bad guys got the money," Caleb told him. "By the time the others got there, it was gone."

Brandon shook his head, then grabbed it and moaned. "Damn, my head hurts. Can't think."

"You don't have to think. You just have to rest. We'll take care of everything," Caleb assured him.

Brandon pulled Caleb closer. "You have to listen. He was here. He said he'd kill you if I didn't give him the money."

Caleb scowled, wondering if he should call the doctor.

"He was *here*," Brandon said again. "I hid the money."

Caleb stared at his partner. "You hid the money? When? Why?"

"After the slide—" He started to cough.

Caleb found a pitcher of water on a nearby tray, poured a little into a cup and held it to Brandon's lips. When his partner seemed to recover, Caleb prompted, "After the slide?"

"I tried to find you but it was dark, raining—got disoriented. I started walking. Ended up back at the compound. Found the bags where we'd thrown them. I was going to put them in the truck, then I heard someone coming. Figured it was one of the Driscoes. I headed back for the forest."

Brandon's voice became drowsy, and his eyes started to close.

Caleb tapped his cheek. "Stay awake, buddy. Tell me what happened."

Brandon looked at him. "I was in no shape to go far. I had to hide the bags."

So Knox's hunch that the Driscoes might not have gotten the money was right. With the drugs stowed in the evidence locker and the money nowhere to be found, Larkin and his boss might just stick around for more than just revenge. "Who shot you, Bran? Was it Larkin?"

"Don't know. I was running for a long time. I heard more than one person coming after me. Maybe two or three. Then I heard shots. Felt this pain in my back."

Probably Larkin taking care of the three of them at once. And not bright enough to check to see if Brandon was dead. Thank God!

"Caleb?"

Caleb looked around. The captain had entered the room. "Yes, sir?"

"Munoz is here."

Good, Caleb thought. There was even more reason now to see Shannon taken to a safe place. "I'll be right out."

He turned to Brandon. "I have to go take care of something. Why don't you rest a minute? I'll be right back."

Apparently exhausted from talking, Brandon nodded and closed his eyes.

As he walked to the conference room, Caleb thought about all Brandon had said. How much of it was real, and how much of it was the product of a fevered mind? Maybe he'd have more of an idea once he went back in, but for now he had to concentrate on convincing one very stubborn woman to go along with his plan to keep her safe.

Opening the door, he heard Sid's voice.

"And then he says, 'But Miss Know-It-All says TV isn't bad for you.'"

Shannon laughed, drawing Caleb's attention to her. Her eyes, too often full of shadows, sparkled like the sun streaming through the leaves to the forest floor. Her face, always lovely, looked young and carefree. He longed to keep that look on her face.

"Seems you have a fan, Shannon," he said.

Sid turned to him. "Hey, Caleb. How's Brandon doing?"

"Hey, Sid," Caleb said, as his gaze caught Shannon's.

The laughter was still in her eyes. For a moment he imagined she was very happy to see him. Maybe one day, he thought, he wouldn't have to imagine it. Maybe once they'd gotten a chance to know each other as more than lovers—which was not to say he wanted to ignore that part of their relationship.

Shannon gazed at Caleb and wondered at the hint of wicked amusement in his blue eyes. "Is your partner going to be all right?"

Caleb moved over to sit by her at the long table. "He's still really tired, but I expect that's normal. I'm going to let him get some rest before I go back in." He glanced at the captain, seated across from him. He would have to tell him what Brandon had said about the money, but he didn't want to discuss it in front of Shannon. It would only worry her. "Can I talk to you and Sid outside for a moment, Captain?"

Before they left the room, Caleb looked at Shannon. "Are you all right here? Can I get you something to drink?"

"I'm fine, Caleb. Captain Gallagher bought me a soda. But I'm in the way here. Why don't I just go home? It's been a long day, and you obviously have better things to do than baby-sit me."

He leaned down and gave her a quick kiss on the lips. "That was a fine speech, honey, but I'm afraid you're just going to have to get used to my taking care of you. Now hold tight, I'll be right back."

SHANNON WAITED until the door closed, then put her arms on the table and laid her head on them. She'd told him! After swearing to go it alone. After telling herself she had no intention of sharing her news with a cop and a stranger. She'd even told him she was grateful for her pregnancy. Why? Had she learned nothing?

Oh, he'd said all the right words. He'd take care of her and their child. He'd handle his job wisely. And he probably meant those vows. But nothing in his hard head seemed to allow for the fact that bad things happened. And they were more likely to happen to people who put themselves in the line of fire.

She tried to believe this would work out. She'd never felt so attracted to a man before. Not even Tony had caused the explosion of feeling she experienced when Caleb touched her.

It was obvious that Caleb was a kind man with deep feelings. And certainly he was a dedicated officer of the law. She sighed wearily. Right now, what she wanted more than anything was to get far, far away from him. Before she started hoping again.

OUT IN THE CORRIDOR, Gallagher and Munoz turned to look at Caleb.

"Brandon told you something, didn't he?" Captain Gallagher asked.

Caleb nodded. "He said he hid the money. Which means Knox's hunch that Larkin and Mick are still around might be right. We have the drugs *and* the money, as far as they're concerned. Bran also said that someone was here and he threatened to kill me if Bran didn't turn it over, but I think that was the medication talking."

"You've been partners for years," Munoz said. "It's normal for him to be concerned about you."

"Yeah, well, I'm concerned about Shannon. Especially since she was followed when she left her cabin last week. Sid, were you able to find out if Larkin owns a two-tone sedan?"

"There's no record of it," Sid said, "but that doesn't mean he doesn't have access to one."

"Well, if it was him," Caleb continued, "he's not going to be a happy camper, letting an amateur lose him. And the fact that Larkin and Mick don't have the money complicates things. Not only do they want me now, but they want the money they think we owe them. We have to put Shannon somewhere they wouldn't think of looking."

Captain Gallagher nodded. "I arranged for a safe house after we talked this afternoon."

"I know that's what we agreed to, Captain, but I've changed my mind." Caleb's gut told him it would be a mistake. 'The Driscoes didn't just suddenly catch on to our undercover operation. They had inside information. If this Mick knew enough to blow our cover, then he'll know enough to figure out the location of any safe houses. I'm sending Shannon someplace I know she'll be safe. Knox and Munoz have already agreed to take her."

"But you haven't told us where that is," Munoz said.

"I will," Caleb said. "After I talk to Shannon."

Munoz's dark eyes widened. "You still haven't told her your plan? What have you been doing the past couple of hours?"

Caleb shrugged and tried to sound casual. "Having lunch, talking. I was about to tell her when I got the call about Brandon. It's probably better this way, anyway. It won't give her so much time to wait and worry."

Captain Gallagher glanced at his watch. "Knox should be here any minute."

Caleb thought he seemed a little nervous. "There's nothing to worry about, Captain."

The captain nodded briskly. "I know. Go ahead and talk to Ms. Garrett."

"I will," Caleb said, not looking forward to the task.

The captain and Munoz grinned at each other.

"You want me and the captain to come help?" Sid offered.

Feeling like a coward, Caleb shook his head. "No, thanks, I think I can handle it just fine," he said, hoping it was true.

"Well, I have a couple of phone calls to make," the captain said. "I'll be out at my car, Munoz. As soon as Knox gets here, we'll finalize plans for moving Ms. Garrett."

Moving Ms. Garrett as if she were a piece of furniture, Caleb thought, instead of the precious mother of his child. But that information was the last thing he wanted to become common knowledge. If Mick and Larkin knew just what Shannon meant to him, she would be in more danger than ever.

Chapter Eleven

The door to the conference room opened, and Shannon lifted her head.

Caleb came in, big and handsome, tough and tender, his dimple flashing. He sat next to her and took her hand. "Trying to get a little shut-eye?" His voice was deep and gentle. "I know it's been a long day for you."

"I'm fine," she snapped, then immediately apologized. "I'm sorry. I guess I'm feeling a little tired and emotional." The urge to lay her head on his wide shoulders and cry her eyes out was almost overwhelming. "I'd really like to go home now."

His grip tightened. "I'm afraid I can't let you do that."

She bristled. "Why not?"

"Because you're not safe on your own. We were under the mistaken impression that the men we're after had the 250 grand Brandon and I were carrying that day. But it turns out Brandon went back after the slide and hid it."

Which gave the bad guys even more reason to stick around, she realized. "I still don't understand what that has to do with me. They'll think you have the

money. It's you they'll want." Which frightened her
down to her toes. It was one thing to think that some-
day she'd lose him to danger; it was quite another to
know just how imminent that danger was.

"You're going to have to trust me on this," Caleb
said.

Trust. There was that word again. Needing some
kind of action, Shannon got up and walked around to
the other side of the table. "Look, Caleb, I'm willing
to acknowledge that you know more about police
work and this particular case than I do, but I'm having
a hard time imagining these men giving me a second
thought. I've already cleared you of the shootings.
Hurting me isn't going to change that."

Caleb rubbed his eyes tiredly. "There's something
about this case you don't know."

She pulled out a chair and sat down. "Such as?"

"We think the Driscoes had inside information,"
he told her.

Shannon's stomach dropped. Bad enough she had
to worry about drug dealers being after him, but now
she had to worry about cops, too? "Do you know
who?"

He shook his head. "No, I've been going over and
over in my head who this Mick guy might be."

She must have looked confused, because he continued, "Right after we got there, Jim Driscoe told
his brother, J.P., to call Mick. We'd only known about
Larkin, who isn't bright enough to have figured we
might be undercover. Besides, there's no other explanation for the Driscoes' sudden knowledge."

She raised a brow. "So you don't know for sure?"

"I know," Caleb said firmly. "When I found out

the Driscoes and Brandon had been shot with my gun, it confirmed my suspicions. I just don't know who.''

''What about Brandon? Is it possible he saw someone, that that's the reason he was shot?''

He shrugged, but there was nothing casual in the movement. ''I'm going to talk to him again as soon as I take care of you.''

She scowled. ''What do you mean by that?''

''I'm sending you to stay with a friend of mine, a retired cop. He's expecting you.''

''Sending me? Aren't you coming with me?'' So he'd be out of harm's way, too, please God.

''Because I'm the only one Bran will talk to, and I think he has more information that will help put this case to rest once and for all.''

''I can wait till you're done talking to him.'' The thought of leaving him now terrified her. What if something happened to him while she was safely hidden with his friend?

''Shannon.''

A single word, yet it held the voices of millions of tough warriors who had to explain to their women why they couldn't stay in the security of their homes.

She crossed her arms. ''So, who gets the pleasure of escorting me?''

''Knox and Munoz.''

''How do you know you can trust them?''

''Malcolm Knox is a longtime veteran of police work. He has the best record in the county. And as for Sid, I'm his daughter's godfather.''

He got up and walked to her side of the table. Once there, he pulled her out of the chair and into his arms. His face was solemn, his eyes warm. ''Please let me take care of you, Shannon. It'll make it so much easier for me to do my job if I know you're safe.''

Tears sprang to her eyes. ''That might be so, but how am I supposed to feel, knowing you're in danger?''

He leaned down and kissed her lips with such tenderness that she longed for the kiss to last forever. Then he drew back. ''Trust me. I can't promise I'll be there to take the training wheels off our little one's first two-wheeler or to see him or her graduate from high school or to hold our first grandchild, but I'll do my best.''

Shannon leaned her head against his chest and breathed in his scent. This man had given her the most precious gift a man could give a woman—his child growing inside her—so the least she could do was give him the trust he needed.

She looked up at him. ''All right, Caleb, I'll go stay at your friend's house, but you have to promise you'll be careful.''

He kissed her on the nose and flashed his dimple. ''You got it, honey.''

There were two quick raps on the door, then Captain Gallagher opened it and stuck his head inside. ''Are you ready?''

''We'll be right there,'' Caleb told him.

Gallagher shut the door.

Caleb put his hands on her shoulders. ''Shannon, there's one other thing.''

His expression was so serious she started to worry again. ''What?''

''I want you to keep the news about your pregnancy to yourself.''

Shannon didn't have to ask why. She knew. If the

bad guys found out that Caleb had a child on the way, it would make him that much more vulnerable.

"Don't worry, Caleb. It will be our secret."

"I won't be able to do this once we walk out the door, so…" He held her close and kissed her hungrily for one brief sizzling moment. "Everything will be okay," he said in a voice husky with emotion. "You'll see."

They walked out of the room to find the three agents waiting for them in the corridor. Captain Gallagher, a commanding figure at any time, had a very serious expression on his face. She didn't blame him, since if what Caleb suspected was correct, it could be one of his men who ruined the undercover operation.

"Shannon," Caleb said, "you've already met my friend, Sid Munoz. I'm sure if you twist his arm, he'll show you pictures of my goddaughter and his terrific son."

Agent Munoz's dark eyes lit up. "You don't even have to go that far," he said charmingly as he shook her hand. "We'll take good care of you, miss."

"And this is Agent Knox."

Shannon turned to face the other man. Except for the cynicism around his eyes, he looked like a television announcer—tall, slender, graying blond hair, just a normal man entering middle age.

"Don't you worry, Ms. Garrett, we'll take good care of you," he said, his tone sincere and competent.

Caleb took her arm. "I'll walk you down to the car to help you get your things and give directions."

The four agents flanked her as they walked her to the parking lot. Without being too obvious, four sets of eyes surveyed the area. Shannon felt a little silly, keeping pace with her protectors. This had to be what the president felt like when he went out, surrounded by Secret Service agents, she thought.

While she got her suitcase out of the Jeep, she heard Caleb give the two agents directions to his friend's place in Moss Landing thirty miles down the coast.

"Ms. Garrett will ride with me," Knox explained to Caleb. "Munoz will stay a couple lengths behind to make sure we're not followed."

Shannon touched Caleb's arm. "Are you sure this is necessary?"

He covered her hand with his. "Yes. I can't concentrate on finding Mick and Larkin if I have to worry about them finding you."

Captain Gallagher stepped forward. "I'm sorry for the inconvenience, Ms. Garrett. We'll get you back to your normal life as soon as possible, I promise."

Normal life? Shannon questioned silently. She didn't think her life would ever be normal again.

WITH ONE HAND gripping Shannon's big floral duffel bag and the other holding her slim hand, Caleb walked Shannon across the parking lot. Her hand trembled a little in his, making him feel even worse about sending her off with the other agents. He tightened his hold. "I'm sorry I can't take you to Dave's place myself."

"It's okay," she said, not looking at him. "I understand you have things that have to be taken care of."

That she didn't like the situation came through loud and clear in the strained tenor of her voice, and he wondered how many times she'd said those same words to her husband.

He wanted to tell her once again that he wasn't Tony, that he wouldn't be reckless. But he kept silent this time. What good were his promises when it came to dealing with a vicious drug ring? Men who sold cocaine to high schoolers would have no qualms about killing an SDU agent. Or the woman he loved.

The thought reverberated so loudly in his brain that he looked over to see if Shannon had heard it. She must have sensed his regard, because she glanced at him. His gaze caught hers. The shadows were back in her eyes, he was sorry to see. But he swore he'd make sure they didn't stay there forever. As soon as all this was over, he would see about bringing the sunshine back into her life.

They arrived at the confiscated vehicles Knox and Munoz were using for their mission.

One was a huge old Chev Impala picked up in a raid of a methamphetamine lab several months before.

Sid went over to stand by the other, a souped-up black Camaro with orange and red flames painted on the sides. "What do you think, Caleb? I swear this was the car of my dreams when I was in high school."

Caleb smiled. "Yeah, well, if I remember right, the teenager who owned this one will be a guest of the California Youth Authority for a few years."

Shannon raised her eyebrows. "Why is that?"

"He was involved in a drive-by shooting," Sid explained. "A rival gang moved into the neighborhood, threatening to take over his gang's very lucrative pot trade."

Too many drugs, Caleb thought. Too many kids in jail. All because people like the Driscoes and Mick and Larkin. Well, he was going to make sure none of it touched his kid. What a crock, he thought. Technically it already had, or he wouldn't be sending his child's mother away.

"I think it's time you got on the road," Captain Gallagher told them. "If you leave now, you should get to Moss Landing before dark."

Reluctantly accepting the inevitable, Caleb opened the passenger door of the ancient Chevy for Shannon. She gave him one long last look. Tension bit the back of his neck as her eyes pleaded, demanded and, in the end, became resigned. She would do as he'd asked. Without a word, she got into the car and stared straight ahead.

Knox walked to the driver's side. "Don't worry, Caleb, we'll take care of your little witness," he said, then he, too, got in.

The old car rumbled to life, and Caleb had to clamp his teeth together to keep from ordering Knox to turn it off and let Shannon out. He didn't want her to go.

Sid clapped him on the back. "Good luck with Brandon. I hope he can help."

Caleb nodded. "Be careful."

Sid sat in the driver's seat of the Camaro of his dreams and grinned. "Of course, buddy, always am."

It was true, Caleb thought. Sid Munoz was careful, competent and completely professional. So why did he find no comfort in that as he watched the cars drive off?

"Ready to go back in?" the captain asked.

"Sure," Caleb said, and meant it. But he couldn't resist another glance at the Impala as it left the parking lot. Shannon would be all right, he told himself. She and their baby would be just fine once they reached Dave's boat.

Back in the hospital, Captain Gallagher went to get coffee, while Caleb returned to Brandon's room.

Caleb studied his dozing partner and noticed how pale and weak he looked. It was still a shock to see his normally healthy friend so beaten up. He hated to wake him, but he had to find out what Brandon knew about the case. The sooner they solved it the better for all concerned.

He pulled up a chair to the bedside and sat. "Brandon? Brandon, wake up."

His partner's eyes opened slowly, much to Caleb's relief.

"Hey, buddy. How ya doin'?"

Brandon tried to smile and failed. "It hurts."

"I'm sorry," Caleb told him. "I should have been there."

"Don't be ridiculous," Brandon scolded.

"You told me a little about what happened. Feel like talking about it?"

Brandon nodded.

"You said you hid the money?"

"In a tree."

Caleb raised his brows. "You climbed a tree?"

Brandon laughed, which turned into a cough.

Caleb poured him a glass of water from the pitcher on the bedside table. "Sorry."

Brandon drank, then handed the glass back to Caleb. "It was a tree trunk, partly burned out in the middle, full of needles. About ten feet tall."

Caleb tried to imagine his partner, in the middle of a rainstorm, on the run from vicious murders, struggling to stuff two backpacks full of money into the trunk of a dead tree. It sounded like a scene from a movie. "You have any idea where this tree trunk is?" Caleb asked.

"Not far from the compound, less than a mile. I'm not really sure which direction."

"Brandon. I know you're ready to drift off again, but there's something else I have to ask you."

His friend nodded sleepily.

"Do you know who shot you?"

"Larkin?"

The doubt in his voice worried Caleb. If not Larkin, who? Mick?

Brandon closed his eyes. "God, I'm tired. Why am I so tired?"

"Because you got run over by a train," Caleb told him, "or the equivalent. Maybe I should go and let you sleep."

"Okay." His eyes flew open. "No, wait!" He grabbed Caleb's arm. "I saw Mick!"

"What?"

"I forgot, my brain's so fuzzy. After I got shot...I fell. But I saw him. Larkin said something to him. Then I saw him before I passed out."

Caleb's heart pounded in his chest. "Did you recognize him? Do we have the guy on file?"

Brandon started to speak, coughed and tried to speak again. "We...we know him. He's one of us."

Caleb's stomach dropped as his fear materialized. "One of us? He's with the SDU? Who?" Damn, he'd hoped he'd been wrong.

He glanced at his watch and thought of Shannon. They should almost be at Dave's by now. He was glad he'd taken the precaution of sending her somewhere safe. He looked at Brandon and saw he'd fallen asleep. "Brandon, wake up! You have to tell me who Mick is."

A nurse walked into the room, then stalked over to stand between him and Brandon. In her sixties, short and plump, she fixed him with a glare that would have terrified a serial killer. "Sir, you'll have to leave now. Mr. Everly is recovering from a serious operation. He needs to rest."

"I understand that, ma'am, but he has important information that I need to know."

"I'm afraid it will have to wait." Her tone said she wasn't going to put up with any of his nonsense.

"It can't. This is a life-or-death matter." A rogue agent could cause far more havoc than any civilian.

"Look, Mr.…." She paused.

"Agent Carlisle," he provided.

"Agent Carlisle, your friend here was in a coma until earlier today. You can't expect him just to get up and run off to help you apprehend criminals."

Caleb decided he was not going to win this clash of wills. Maybe it was time to try charm. He smiled. "I understand how serious Brandon's condition is, but he'll tell you himself how important this is, if you'll just let me wake him up."

She crossed her arms in front of her ample chest.

"I'm impervious to your wishes, young man. My patient's welfare comes first." She turned her head to look at Brandon. "Look at your friend, Agent Carlisle. Do you want him to have a relapse?"

Caleb shook his head. "Of course not, but—"

"But nothing. You're just going to have to wait. Now, are you going to leave or do I have to call Security?"

Caleb didn't see any point in arguing. "No, ma'am, I'll leave."

He walked out the door. Officer Reedley was sitting at his station just outside the door. It occurred to Caleb that his partner might be in more danger from outside forces than from his injuries. Brandon was the only one who could identify Mick. "Reedley, I'm going to go find Captain Gallagher. Do not, I repeat, do not let anyone but me into this room. Do you understand?"

"Yes, sir."

Caleb gave him a short nod, then went off to find the captain. Maybe he could convince the nurse's superiors to call off the guard dog and let him talk to Brandon. If Mick got to him first, a relapse was the least of their worries.

Following the signs that pointed to the cafeteria, Caleb thought of Shannon and the circumstances that had brought her into his life. He hadn't asked for it. Certainly hadn't expected it. But now he couldn't imagine being with anyone else. He just hoped she felt the same way about him, even though he was the one who'd gotten her into this mess.

Well, he told himself as he arrived at his destination, at least she was safely away from it now.

HIGHWAY ONE NORTH just past Watsonville, where the four-lane road narrowed to two, was congested with commuter traffic. Not wanting to bother Agent Knox when he needed to concentrate on driving, Shannon looked out the window at the scenery. Green hills towered over rolling farmland, both shadowed by dark clouds moving in from the west. Brisk winds buffeted homeward-bound vehicles, but the big Impala never budged. It was a quality that reminded her of Caleb.

A reminder she hadn't really wanted. It was hard enough trying to keep herself from worrying about him. He was going after that money. He would have to. He'd already felt responsible for the disastrous operation that had left his partner injured, several men dead and 250 thousand dollars unaccounted for. She just hoped he'd be careful as he'd promised. For the baby's sake. And, she had to admit if only to herself, for her sake.

"Munoz must be going crazy having to hold that Camaro at a snail's pace."

Knox's comment drew her attention away from thoughts of Caleb. She shook her head in bewilderment. "Men and their toys. I'll never understand it."

"Are you saying women don't like nice cars?"

"Not for the same reasons," she offered, glad to have an innocuous conversation to take her mind off her concerns. "Most women don't see their car as an extension of themselves."

"Sounds like you've done some research on the subject, Miss Know-It-All," he teased.

A little surprised, she smiled. Agent Knox didn't seem like the teasing type. "It comes with the job, I'm afraid."

They reached the salt marshes just south of Moss Landing. Shannon looked out at the birds that picked among the cattails and waded in the shallow water looking for food. A white egret rose from the tall weeds, flying off on graceful wings. Looking for new territory, she guessed.

The thought struck a chord deep within her memory. Looking for new territory. Who said that? Tony?

It had to be. It seemed like a phrase he would use—had used, she remembered—when talking about someone he knew who'd left town. "Criminals never change. They just move on to new territory."

But it wasn't a criminal he'd been talking about. Who was it? Suddenly it seemed very important she remember.

"Is something wrong?" Agent Knox asked.

"No," Shannon told him. But it was a lie. Something was wrong. If only she could figure out why that phrase about looking for new territory had triggered her memory.

"You probably just need some food and a good night's sleep. We're almost there." Knox flipped on his blinker.

Shannon saw a sign that said Zmudowski State Beach ahead on the right.

Knox made the turn, confusing her. "I didn't know there were residences down this way."

The agent shrugged. "These are the directions I was given."

There was a hard note in his voice Shannon hadn't noticed before. Something wasn't right. Agent Knox seemed too serious.

She saw him check the rearview mirror. A prickle of fear feathered the back of her neck. Could someone be following them?

She twisted around to see out the back window. Caleb believed that the man who'd followed her to Monterey could have been one of the men he was after. She scanned the road for a two-toned sedan. But the only car she could see was the one driven by Agent Munoz.

She sat straight again, trying to convince herself

there was nothing to worry about. She glanced over at Agent Knox. He, too, seemed to be keeping an extra eye on the rearview mirror.

They reached the end of the long narrow road they'd been traveling. Zmudowski Beach. She'd been there a time or two years before. The water of the bay looked slate-gray in the dying light of early evening.

On the left lay a parking lot with a lone car in it. She squinted, trying to see if there was someone in it. But it was parked in the shadow of a Monterey cypress, and she could barely make it out. Knox pulled into the lot. For a moment the headlights shone on the parked car. Shannon's breath caught. The two-toned sedan.

Knox stopped the car and switched off the ignition. He turned to face her. The sliver of sun that shone through the clouds was behind him, so she couldn't see his face clearly.

"It's too bad what happened to your husband," he said.

Her heart seemed to stop beating, then resumed at a much faster pace. "You knew my husband?"

"No, just did some checking into your background," he replied silkily. "Seems like old Tony was pretty reckless."

Something was going on here. Something she didn't like. But what? "Is there some point to discussing my past?"

Knox smiled. "No. No point at all."

He was lying. "If you have something to say, Agent Knox, maybe you should come out and say it."

"No beating around the bush for you, eh, Miss Know-It-All?" Knox replied dryly.

Shannon waited. The man was playing a game only he knew the rules to.

When she didn't say anything, he nodded. "Well, since you asked. I just thought it was rather ironic you went from one reckless cop to another."

"I don't know what you mean," Shannon said, feeling as if she was in the middle of a nightmare, or Alice's Wonderland. Nothing seemed to fit.

Knox's eyes glinted. "Nice try, Ms. Garrett, but we both know you're smarter than that." His tone was dead serious now. "I know you and Carlisle are lovers. If you want him to live, you'd better cooperate."

Chapter Twelve

Caleb! Shannon wanted to scream, to cry, to hit out at this man who threatened to take away her baby's father.

The baby! No. God, no, he couldn't find out about the baby. If he knew, Caleb wouldn't have a chance.

She took a deep breath, trying to steady her jangled nerves. There had to be something she could do. There had to be some way out of this.

Agent Munoz.

She looked around for the Camaro and saw it drive into the lot. Munoz had a wife and children. Caleb was his daughter's godfather. Surely he wasn't in on it.

"No, he's not," Knox said as if reading her mind. "He'll have to be taken care of, too."

We'll take care of your little witness, he'd reassured Caleb. The words had sounded odd to her at the time. Now she knew why.

Over Knox's shoulder, she saw a man get out of the sedan and walk toward Sid Munoz, who had parked a couple of spaces away. The man raised something over his head and brought it down on Munoz's.

"Noooo!" Shannon screamed.

The agent lay crumpled on the ground.

"Oh my God. He's killed him."

Knox didn't even bother to turn around. "I doubt it. Larkin rarely disobeys my orders. Although he did foolishly fail when told not to let you out of his sight last week. No, I need Munoz alive, just in case my original plan doesn't hold up."

She didn't want to ask, but she had to know. "What *is* your original plan?"

Knox smiled. "Let's just say it involves you and the brave Agent Carlisle. Dedicated to law enforcement and dedicated to you, just like your husband. You do know how to pick 'em, Miss Know-It-All."

CALEB, ALONG WITH Captain Gallagher, waited impatiently outside the door of his partner's room. Brandon's doctor had insisted on examining him before allowing Caleb to talk to him again.

Leaning against the wall, Caleb shifted to take the weight off his still-sore ankle. He stuck his hands in the front pockets of his jeans. Inaction made him restless. Not being able to contact Shannon was driving him crazy. Where was she? Nearly at Dave's? She had to be.

He glanced over at the captain, who sat in a nearby chair, elbows on knees, staring down at his brown suede shoes. Anyone looking at him would think he was just a worried family member. Closer study would reveal deeper emotion. His hands were balled into fists. A vein throbbed at his temple. His mouth was drawn tight. There was anger there, and frustration.

"Who do you think it is, Captain?" Caleb asked.

The other man looked up at him. "I don't have a clue. I wish to hell I did." He rose and moved over to stand by Caleb. "I keep trying to figure out why someone would go rogue like this. It isn't just keeping a little of the evidence on the sly. This man is trafficking. He'd know the consequences. Who the hell in my department would be arrogant enough or stupid enough not to figure on getting caught?"

"Someone who needs the money," Caleb speculated aloud. "Bills to pay, a family to take care of." It didn't sound right. As the captain had said, this scum was involved in drug smuggling. Big bucks. Mega bucks. This was more than trying to make a house payment or pay for Johnny's braces.

"I can't imagine any of the family men we know doing something like this."

"No," Gallagher agreed. "It takes more than trying to balance a budget to drive someone over to the other side."

"Which means we're back to arrogance and greed. Greed makes people reckless."

"Yeah, but there doesn't seem to be a lot of recklessness here," Gallagher mused. "This guy's covered his tracks all the way. Hell, the only mistake he made that I can see is he forgot to make sure Everly was dead."

"Thank God for that." Caleb couldn't imagine working without his friend and partner.

The captain nodded. "I'll second that."

The doctor came out of Brandon's room. "I'll give you five minutes with your partner, Agent Carlisle. His condition seems stable, but it's iffy as to whether it'll stay that way, so don't upset him."

"Thanks, Dr. Powell," Caleb said. "I'll be careful."

Back in the hospital room, Caleb pulled up a chair so Brandon wouldn't have to strain to look up at him. "Hey, buddy, the doctor says you're doing okay."

"Easy for him to say."

In spite of the humor, his friend's voice sounded strained.

"I won't take long," Caleb told him. "When I was here before, you told me you had seen someone right after you fell, someone who was one of us. Can you tell me what you meant? Who did you see?"

"Mi…" His voice failed. Brandon cleared his throat. "I saw Mick."

"Yes," Caleb said patiently. "Did you recognize him? Do you know who Mick is?"

"Not Mick. M.I.K." He spoke slowly. "Malcolm I. Knox."

Caleb felt as if he'd been kicked in the stomach. His heart pounded. He grabbed Brandon's arm. "Knox? You're sure it was Knox?"

"I'm sure," Brandon said. "Why? What's wrong?"

Caleb covered his face with his hands. What was wrong? Everything. It had been Knox all along. Knox, the twenty-year veteran. Knox, the hard-boiled agent. Knox, the man he'd trusted with the woman he loved, the mother of his child.

He got up and strode to the door. "Captain, get in here."

SITTING IN THE CAR which now reeked of cigarette smoke, Shannon clasped her hands tightly in her lap and tried to keep calm. Panicking wasn't going to get her anywhere. It would help, probably, if she had some idea of Knox's plan for her and Caleb.

She looked over at him. He was looking out the window at the man who'd hit Agent Munoz. She did the same. If she got away from these men, she wanted to be able to describe them to the police.

The man, who was crouched next to the agent's unmoving form, was tall and very thin, with dirty-blond hair and a scraggly beard. He looked just what she'd expect a drug dealer to look like. In essence, the complete opposite of Knox, who had the distinguished good looks of a news anchor or college professor.

Which just proved that you couldn't tell a book by its cover. The man was scum. If she didn't find some way to foil him, he'd kill Caleb.

It wasn't fair. Her baby deserved a father. And, God knows, she needed him. The thought of losing him nearly undid her.

She watched as the other man stood and walked over to the Impala. Knox rolled down his window. "Larkin."

"He'll be out for a while. What do you want me to do with him?"

The nervous whiny tone of his voice grated on Shannon's already jangled nerves.

"Cuff his hands behind him," Knox ordered, "then drag him over here. We'll put him in the trunk."

Larkin went off to do as he was ordered.

Knox turned to her. "As soon as we put Agent Munoz to bed, we'll be on our way."

The casual tone of his statement frightened her more than any overt threat.

"Why are you doing this?" she asked quietly, longing for Caleb to come, longing even more for him to stay away.

Knox smiled. "Money problems, sweetheart. The people who provided the merchandise for the buy last week don't just give it away. They expect to be paid. Unfortunately, due to those idiot Driscoes, there's no money to pay them."

If he expected her to be sympathetic to his plight, he could think again, Shannon thought. "I meant, why would a respected SDU agent traffic in drugs? Caleb told me you have the best arrest record in the state."

He reached for the door handle. "Good way to get rid of the competition, don't you think?" He opened the door and stepped out.

A chill wind blew through, making her shiver. She had to get away from this man. Once he had his money, he'd kill her. There was no doubt in her mind.

She heard a buzzing sound and realized he'd left the keys in the ignition. She tried to calculate how long it would take her to scoot behind the wheel and start the car.

Knox leaned down to peer inside. "Oh, Shannon?"

She looked at him.

He'd taken his weapon from his shoulder holster and aimed it at her. "Don't even think about doing anything stupid." Then he reached in and grabbed the keys.

AFTER BRANDON CONFIRMED for the captain what he'd just revealed to him, Caleb told his partner he'd see him later and made a call to his friend Dave, which confirmed the nonarrival of the two agents and

Shannon. Subsequent calls to Munoz and Knox went unanswered. Captain Gallagher put out an APB for both vehicles, then put in calls to off-duty agents. He ordered Caleb to stay put, but Caleb refused.

Gallagher caught up to him halfway down the hall. "I'm going to call the FBI."

Caleb shrugged. "Do what you have to. Just don't expect me to hang around until they show up."

He strode down another hall, across the lobby, then exited the hospital through the automatic doors. Gallagher kept up with him every step of the way.

"Where are you going?"

"I'm going to take Shannon's Jeep, drive to Moss Landing and hope to God I find them."

"Then what?" the older man demanded.

Then he was going to beat the crap out of Knox, he thought.

"I'm sending backup with you."

Caleb shrugged. "Sure. Just tell them to stay out of my way."

"Do you think Munoz is in on this?"

Caleb swung around, fists clenched. "No!"

The captain nodded. "Neither do I."

So how would Knox get away with a detour to somewhere other than their planned destination? Caleb wondered as he unlocked the Jeep. A fake engine problem? Or maybe he'd just have Larkin run Sid off the road. Larkin had to be involved in this. Or maybe one of his other fellow agents?

Feeling weary, Caleb rubbed the back of his neck. "You know the worst thing about all this? It's people we've worked with for years." He got in the Jeep, then looked back at the captain. "Now we don't know who to trust."

The captain put a hand on his shoulder. "Trust yourself, Carlisle."

Caleb nodded, then closed the door and turned on the ignition. Trust yourself, the captain had said. Good advice, if you weren't responsible for putting the woman carrying your child into the care of a murdering traitor.

KNOX AND HIS PAL Larkin put Agent Munoz in the trunk, while Shannon tried desperately to come up with a plan of escape. The sun had set and fog was creeping in. The parking lot, deserted except for them, was surrounded by sand dunes. To the west beyond the beach and rocks lay Monterey Bay. A mile or so to the east lay the highway, which was surely her best bet. The problem would be making it across the parking lot without getting shot.

She looked toward the road, hoping someone would come. It was getting dark. A ranger or someone would be coming by to chain off the lot sooner or later, she suspected, but would she still be here? Maybe in the trunk with Munoz?

Her door opened, startling her.

"Let's go," Knox ordered.

She saw no smile on his face now, only a glimpse of the criminal under the cop facade. She didn't dare question him. She had more than her own safety to think of.

He grabbed her arm and led her over to the sedan. Up close she could see it was faded charcoal and gray. He opened the back door and pushed her inside. Larkin was already there.

"Watch her," he ordered, then slammed the door.

A few seconds later he got in the driver's seat and turned on the ignition.

Shannon sat as far to the left side of the car as she could. She didn't want to be anywhere near Knox's grungy-looking flunky.

Knox put the car into gear and accelerated out of the parking lot. Within minutes, they were headed north on Highway One.

Shannon hoped that it wouldn't be long before someone found the abandoned cars, and that when they did, they checked the trunk of the Impala. Agent Munoz would need medical attention.

It was obvious that Knox was kidnapping her. He needed the money that had gotten lost during Caleb's fight with the drug dealers. Knox would offer her in return for the cash. But then what?

"You've stopped asking questions, Ms. Garrett," Knox said. "Aren't you interested in what's going to happen to you?"

Larkin laughed, a sniveling sound that made her hope he was as stupid as he sounded. It might come in handy later.

"I'm interested," she said evenly. It took a lot of effort to keep sarcasm out of her voice.

"Well, it's not my intention to hurt you. As long as you behave yourself."

She saw the sign announcing the turnoff for Pajaro Valley Golf Course. She knew there was a traffic light at that intersection. She glanced quickly at the door and noticed that Knox hadn't locked it. She would only need a minute. There were plenty of cars around, plenty of people to run to for help.

Then she remembered. Jumping out of the car

when it slowed for a stoplight wasn't an option, not when there was the possibility of harming her child.

"Do we understand each other?" Knox asked.

"Yes."

"Good. Now my other problem is where to leave you while I contact your lover."

She clenched her hands at Knox's snide tone. He made her time with Caleb sound dirty, when it was so wonderful. Then she noticed him observing her reaction in the rearview mirror.

Knox laughed silkily. "Surprised I figured it out? That'll teach you to underestimate me. Too bad all the others never figured it out."

"Caleb won't let you get away with this," she snapped, unable to keep herself from reacting to his arrogance.

"And just how do you think he's going to stop me, Miss Know-It-All?"

She didn't answer. It had been a stupid thing to say aloud. Still, she believed it with all her heart.

"Carlisle is very good at what he does," Knox said nastily, "but not as good as I am. He has one flaw that will help me win this round—he cares about you. It'll make him sloppy."

Maybe a lesser man, Shannon thought. Not the man who'd survived a landslide to walk miles in the pouring rain, injured and bleeding. He hadn't given up that night. He hadn't given up on his partner recovering. He wouldn't give up on her.

"So where we takin' her, Knox?" Larkin asked.

"A place I know in the mountains." His gaze shifted from the road ahead to the rearview mirror again. He smiled the smile of a man totally satisfied with his own ingenuity.

And it hit Shannon. Knox was taking her to her cabin.

CALEB WAS HALFWAY to Moss Landing when he got the news on his cell phone that both vehicles had been located in the parking lot at Zmudowski State Beach. Wishing for lights and a siren, he hit the accelerator, praying all the way that Shannon and Sid were there, safe and unharmed.

Twelve eternal minutes later, he drove into the parking lot to find two sheriff's vehicles at the scene, alongside the cars Knox and Munoz had been driving.

He went over to the Camaro, looked through the window, saw nothing, then proceeded to the Impala. His heart thumped as he viewed the interior. Again nothing. At least Knox hadn't killed her. At least not here. "Damn, he took her with him."

One of the deputies came up to him. "Can I help you, sir?"

"Carlisle, SDU." Caleb showed him his badge.

"Hendrick," the deputy said. "I was told you'd be here." The other deputy approached. Hendrick introduced him as Rodriguez. "The Department got an anonymous call about twenty minutes ago that something was going on in the parking lot. We'd received the APB just minutes before the call."

Knox, damn him, Caleb thought. The scum wanted him to know he had Shannon and Sid.

"There were no signs of anyone around, and both vehicles are locked. We have a slim-jim if you wanna take a look."

"Thanks," Caleb said. "Let's try the Impala first."

Deputy Rodriguez slid in the instrument. Seconds

later the lock clicked and he opened the driver's-side door.

Caleb leaned over to look inside.

"Here, you'll need this."

He took the proffered flashlight from Hendrick, then went to work searching the front for some kind of ransom note. Knox had made it a point to call in the whereabouts of the abandoned cars. There had to be a reason.

Finding nothing in the front seat, he moved to the back, where he found Shannon's purse jammed under the back of driver's seat. He grabbed it and dumped out the contents. Wallet, brush, makeup, checkbook, tissues and various other items spilled over the seat. But nothing to indicate where Knox had taken her.

He opened her wallet. Behind a transparent plastic window was her California driver's license. He gazed down at her smiling face, and his heart hurt. How could he have been so careless with her?

"Find something, Carlisle? That belong to someone you know?"

Caleb nodded. Someone he knew. Someone he'd fallen in love with. Someone carrying his child. Someone he'd sent off with the devil.

A dull thud interrupted his thoughts. He sat stock-still, listening. Thud! There it was again. "The trunk!" He climbed out of the back seat. "Someone's in the trunk. Hit the release," he ordered the others.

He rushed to the back of the car. The lid popped open. A dim light illuminated the inside—and the straining form of his bound and gagged friend. "Sid!" To the deputies he called, "Help me!"

Between the three of them, they got Sid out and released his bonds, then laid him on the ground.

Sid groaned and reached for his head.

"Are you hurt?" Caleb felt the back of his head and located a huge lump. Someone had obviously hit him from behind. Caleb took off his jacket and made a pillow. "Get a blanket and call the paramedics," he ordered. Then he turned back to his friend.

"Sid, I know you're hurting, but I need to know what happened to Shannon."

The agent opened his eyes and gazed up at him, his expression tortured. "I'm sorry."

Fear raced through him. "Sorry. Sorry for what? Where's Shannon?"

"I don't know." He reached up to hold his head, then continued, his voice strained, "We were almost to Moss Landing when Knox turned off on the Zmudowski Beach road. I tried to raise him on the phone, but I kept getting a busy signal. So I followed him. He pulled into the lot. I got out of the car to find out what was going on. The light was fading, and I didn't even see the guy who hit me. That's the last thing I remember, until I woke up in the trunk." He reached for Caleb. "Did he get Knox and Shannon, too?"

Caleb grabbed his hand. "They didn't get Knox. Knox got Shannon. I talked to Brandon. Knox is Mick."

Sid's eyes widened. "No."

Caleb nodded. "Yes. It's been him all along. Now he's after the money."

He heard the sound of a siren in the distance. "Listen, pal, you're going to be all right. The ambulance will be here in a second, but I have to go. I have to find her."

"I understand," Sid said. "But do you have any idea where he'd take her?"

"None," Caleb admitted painfully.

The agent closed his eyes. Caleb thought he'd fallen unconscious and began to worry. "Sid?"

"The hills."

Caleb frowned. "What?"

His friend opened his eyes, now hot and intense. "The hills. That's where it happened. That's where he'll take her."

Yes, Caleb thought. It only made sense. The money was there somewhere. But why bother to drag a woman along when he went to look for it?

Then he realized. Knox wouldn't. He had no intention of looking for the money himself. Why should he when he had a hostage? All he had to do was sit back and wait for Caleb to bring the money to him.

Bring it to him where?

Then it hit him. Shannon's cabin! What better place?

As soon as he got back on the highway, Caleb called in to Gallagher. "He's holding her at the cabin. I know it."

"I'll send men up there."

A steely determination came over him. "No. I'm going alone." He felt for the gun, which he'd taken from one of the deputies, now tucked into his waistband.

"You'll need assistance."

"Dammit, Captain, we've been through this before. I can't do my job if I'm worried about my back."

"The FBI—"

"—will just get in the way," Caleb interrupted. "I can't take the chance. This is my woman. I have to do this my way."

"You're too close to this. Personal involvement makes a cop reckless."

Reckless, Caleb thought, remembering Shannon's accusations. But he knew this had nothing to do with recklessness and everything to do with making sure the woman he loved didn't suffer for his mistakes. "I just found her, Captain. I'm not going to lose her now."

"Carlisle—"

"I'll handle it, Captain. No one else has as much stake in seeing this through." No one else knew there was the child, as well as the woman, to think of. "I've spent time at the cabin. I'll let you know if I need help."

He hung up, tossed the phone on the passenger seat and jammed his foot on the gas. And once Shannon was safe, he would make Knox pay for what he'd done. For the drugs, for the kidnapping, for the murders, for the betrayal of the code he'd vowed to live by.

What if the bastard had hurt Shannon? A shard of fear lodged in his heart. What if she was already d—

He cut off the thought as it formed. He couldn't think of that. Panic would only eat at his confidence, leave him unable to do the job he had to do. He had to believe she was unharmed. He had to believe he would get to her in time. For once in his life, he was so close to getting the family he'd always wanted. He was not going to lose them.

Chapter Thirteen

As KNOX DROVE UP the winding road that led to her cabin, Shannon studied the moonlit landscape with new eyes. She no longer saw the forest as the comfortable refuge she'd come to know. Nerves on edge, she knew these trees would witness her death if she didn't find an escape route.

She couldn't help wondering why Knox had taken her here. Wouldn't being in a familiar area give her more of a chance to escape?

Maybe that's what he's counting on, Shannon. Maybe he's thinking you'll be overconfident. Maybe he's just waiting for you to make that mistake.

Her confidence waned and panic threatened. She took a deep breath. *You can get through this, Shannon. You just have to be calm. That's the only way you'll get out of this mess.*

Being in familiar territory did give her more of a chance. Knox didn't know his way around here the way she did. All she needed were a few seconds of inattention and she'd be gone. She could hide out in the woods all night and he'd never find her.

Knox brought the car to a stop in front of her cabin. He looked at her in the rearview mirror. "Glad to be home, sweetheart?'' Without waiting for an answer, he opened his door.

It was a good thing, too. She was finding it harder and harder to keep her mouth shut. During the hour it had taken to drive here, her patience had been tried nearly to its limits by Knox's arrogance and Larkin's grating laugh.

Her door swung open.

''Let's go,'' Knox ordered.

She got out and took another deep breath. A breeze blew up suddenly, freshening the air. She heard a whoosh of wings, then the hoot of an owl. Another night bird called, a strange cry that sounded like ''Caleb.'' It was only a trick of her imagination, but it strengthened her resolve. Caleb would come. She had to be ready to help him.

''Where's the key?''

Knox's demand claimed her attention. She contemplated telling him she didn't have one with her, which was true. But Knox would simply order Larkin to break in.

She walked in front of him and went up the steps of the front porch to a plastic-covered wicker rocker. She pulled up the plastic, then reached under the cushion and retrieved her spare key. She turned and handed it to Knox.

''You're a smart girl, Miss Know-It-All. Keep it that way.''

He handed the key to Larkin. ''Open the door.''

With a nervous giggle, Larkin did as he was told.

Knox motioned for her to follow him inside.

Entering her home for the first time in eight days, Shannon was hit point-blank in the heart with mem-

ories of making love to Caleb. The feeling was unexpected and completely unnerving.

She'd lived in the cabin for three years. It had always been hers, only hers. Now, after spending a
mere twenty-four hours with Caleb, it was *theirs*. Everywhere she looked, she was reminded of Caleb's
touch, his kisses, his hands. She nearly groaned aloud
with wanting. Though the fireplace held nothing but
blackened ashes and the cabin was chilly, Shannon's
body felt hot, her face flushed.

"Tie her to one of the kitchen chairs."

Knox's order washed over her like a bucket of ice
water. It had been a long drive, and it seemed there'd
be no letup on the fear Knox had instilled in her when
he'd made it clear she would be used as a bargaining
chip in this frightening game of his. "Would you
mind if I used the bathroom first?" she asked as po-
litely as she could manage. Knox's increasing sarcasm indicated an instability of personality. She
didn't want to see what would happen if she tested
it.

"I'll take you. Larkin, find a rope. I want her well
secured." He grabbed Shannon's arm. "Let's go."

His fingers bit into her flesh through the soft
sweater, the first sign of the rough handling to come
if she didn't behave.

With Knox waiting on the other side of the door,
Shannon took as long as she could in the bathroom.
Thinking. Planning. Trying not to panic. *Caleb, where
are you?*

There was no way she could fit through the tiny
window above the bathtub. Knox had checked before
he'd left her alone. She quickly searched her medicine
cabinet and the cabinet beneath the sink for anything

useful. Her disposable razor was only good for nicking her legs.

Knox pounded on the door. "Time's up, sweetheart. Move it."

When she emerged, he grabbed her arm and escorted her back to the kitchen, where Larkin was waiting with the rope she'd kept in one of the cupboards "just in case." Just in case of what, she'd never quite figured out. It certainly hadn't occurred to her that one day it would be used to tie her to one of her own kitchen chairs.

Knox pushed her into the seat. "Tie her up and do it right. I'm going to look around." With that, he walked out the door.

As Larkin yanked on the rope, making it bite into her wrist, she yelped.

"Shut up," he ordered.

"The rope's too tight," she snapped back. "You're cutting off my circulation."

'So what? You're not going anywhere." He giggled at his lame witticism.

Knox slammed back into the cabin. "What the hell is going on in here?"

Larkin's ugly pointy face sobered. "She keeps whining that the rope's too tight."

"So loosen it," Knox said. He walked over and touched her face, making her shudder with revulsion. "We wouldn't want you to be uncomfortable during your long wait, would we, sweetheart."

She contemplated spitting in his swarmy face, then decided that wouldn't be such a great idea.

He grinned as if he knew just what she was thinking. "Well, now that you're taken care of, sweetheart,

I'm afraid I'm going to have to leave you with Larkin.''

She glanced over at the mangy mutt of a man and shuddered again. She looked back at Knox. "Where are you going?"

He raised a brow. "It's none of your business, but I admire your impudence in asking."

Though she was shaking inside, she affected a bored expression. "What should I tell Caleb when he comes?"

Knox shot her a ferocious look and didn't reply. He turned to Larkin. "Watch her and keep your gun close," he said with more than a touch of sarcasm. "She's a smart one." He laughed again. "Miss Know-It-All, indeed." He stuck his hand in his jacket pocket.

Shannon's stomach clenched. Was he going for his gun? Did he intend to kill her now?

When he pulled his hand out, it took everything in her not to flinch.

"I need you to do something for me, sweetheart."

In his hand was a small tape recorder.

Relief flowed through her, until she realized what he wanted her to do. He was going to use her voice to get to Caleb. And once he had her voice on tape, would he still need her?

"All you have to do is say, 'Caleb, Caleb, please help me.'"

She gritted her teeth together.

He turned on the recorder. "Say it," he ordered.

Tears threatened. Shannon willed them back and prayed. *Please, God, don't let him kill me. Please save my baby.*

"Now!" Knox yelled.

She took a deep breath and said the words.

"That's better."

Then he left.

Hearing the car drive away, Shannon allowed herself to breathe. She was still alive. Her baby still had a chance, she told herself. Caleb would come. There was no way someone as arrogant as Knox would outwit the man who'd stolen her heart. Caleb would come.

DAMN! CALEB SMACKED the steering wheel of the Jeep as he neared the Scott's Valley exit. How could he have missed it? He'd spent the past week going through the personnel records of every agent on the payroll. Including Knox. There'd been nothing. No clue.

"And you call yourself a cop," he sneered at himself.

The low fuel warning chime sounded as he took the exit. Since the light had been on for a while, he decided he couldn't ignore it any longer. He was only about twenty-five minutes from Shannon's, but the vehicle wouldn't do them any good if it ran out of gas.

Besides, he'd already made enough stupid mistakes.

He stopped at a self-serve station, then stuck the nozzle into the tank and started it. He paced as he waited for the tank to fill. God, he hoped he was right about this.

Knox taking Shannon to her place made sense because of its proximity to the compound. Knox might be scum, but he wasn't stupid. Unless he'd had this planned from the beginning—and Caleb didn't see how he could have—Knox had to think fast. Shannon's cabin was only logical.

The thought of Shannon held captive in her own cabin knotted in his gut. She didn't deserve this. And she'd never have been involved if he hadn't used her to clear himself.

He wished Brandon was here. His partner would have steadied him. He was the smartest man Caleb knew. *And he would have cracked you over the head for the self-pity party you're having, Carlisle,* he scolded himself. His fault or not, Shannon was in trouble. He had to put feelings aside and act like a professional. Because it was the cop who could save her, not the man who couldn't get enough of her.

Caleb reached back to rub the tension from the back of his neck. He closed his eyes for a moment to visualize the road to the cabin. He'd only been on it once, but he seemed to remember there being a couple of places within walking distance where he could stash the Jeep.

The gas nozzle clicked, and Caleb walked over to take it out. A twinge in his ankle reminded him of his recent injury, but he deliberately ignored it. He'd hike up the mountain if he had to.

When he got back into the Jeep, he noticed the cell phone he had left on the dashboard. He picked it up and flipped it open. The LCD display indicated he'd missed two incoming calls. "Damn!" Hurriedly he punched the call log button.

Suddenly the phone rang. "Carlisle," he answered.

"You're a hard man to get hold of," Knox's voice taunted. "This is my third try. I would have thought under the circumstances you would have kept your cell phone in your pocket."

"Knox, if you've hurt her..."

"Where are you, Carlisle?"

An ambulance, siren screaming, sped by, giving him an idea. If Knox didn't know he was in the area...

"Moss Landing. The paramedics just left to take Sid to the hospital." That ought to buy him some time.

"Oh, he's still alive, then?"

The bored tone sent Caleb's blood pressure rocketing. "Yes, you bastard, no thanks to you."

"Larkin does the dirty work. I just give the orders."

"Where's Shannon?"

"Somewhere safe, as long as you do what I say."

"You slimy—"

"Uh-uh-uh, Carlisle, no name calling. I'm the one in charge now."

He was right, Caleb thought. He couldn't afford to provoke the man, not when Shannon's life was at stake. "Knox, why are you doing this?"

"Hey, I'm just looking out for number one."

"By kidnapping an innocent woman?"

"You can give the credit for that to your partner. He should have left my money alone. Now it's up to you to get it for me, or your little Miss Know-It-All will be little Miss Dead."

Caleb closed his eyes and said a brief prayer. *Please help me make this work, God.* He took a breath and lied, "Brandon can't remember where he put it. But I can make arrangements for more. It's just going to take some time."

"Nice try, Carlisle, but I'm not buying it. I want

the money you brought to the compound in back-packs. No substitutes.''

Caleb frowned. What difference did it make what money he got? ''You have to know, Knox, that Captain Gallagher has already called in the FBI.''

Knox laughed. ''Has he? Well, I'm sure you'll keep them out of it. If you want your sweetheart back alive.''

''My sweetheart?'' Knox couldn't know how close they were.

Knox laughed. ''I'm trained to observe, Carlisle, just like you. I knew the minute you came back that something had happened between you two. And it certainly didn't take an Einstein to figure out why you've been moping around the office the past week. When you asked me to transport her to safety, you handed me my insurance policy.''

And for that, Caleb knew, he'd never forgive himself. ''Fine, then, how do I get her back?''

''The money—''

''If you hurt her—''

''As soon as I have what I need, I'll be on my way. We'll both have what we want. You get the girl. I get my money. You won't see me again.''

There wasn't an airport or major freeway that wasn't being watched as they spoke. And if Knox was smart enough to find another route? Well, they'd catch the bastard. Eventually. Caleb would see to it.

But what would Knox have done to Shannon by that time? Caleb shuddered at the thought.

''It'll take you about an hour to get to the Driscoe compound. I'll give you another thirty minutes to find the backpack and my money.''

''That's not enough time.'' Caleb protested. ''It's

dark, and I told you, Brandon couldn't tell me where he hid it.''

''There's an old saying about a job expanding with the time you take to do it,'' Knox said. ''If you want to see your girlfriend alive…well, you know the drill.''

''I want to talk to Shannon.''

''No.''

''Knox! I need to hear her voice. I need to know she's okay.''

''Oh, all right.''

Caleb scowled. Had Knox just given in way too easily?

''Caleb? Caleb, please help me.''

''Shannon?''

''Wait for my call,'' Knox ordered, and hung up.

Caleb sat for a moment trying to figure out why Shannon had sounded so odd. It was almost as if she'd been reading a script.

He started the Jeep. It didn't matter. He'd bought himself an hour. Time enough to get her away from Knox and retrieve the money. Before turning onto the winding road that led to the cabin, Caleb turned off the headlights.

The wind had blown the clouds away, enabling him to negotiate the remaining distance by moonlight. About a mile from the driveway, he pulled the Jeep over, parking it between two redwood trees. Keeping to the side of the road, he walked about a half mile, then he turned off and started hiking uphill through the trees.

His ankle gave him a twinge or two, but adrenaline and thoughts of Shannon drove him on through the dark forest. It amazed him how much his life had

changed in the past ten days. Until he'd arrived at
Shannon's door that night, his job had been his life.
Now, because of her, he was going to have a family.
And because of his assumption that Knox was the
good agent he'd always been painted, he might never
get to enjoy it.

It didn't matter that Shannon wasn't his wife and
their baby wasn't much past the twinkle-in-her-
mother's-eye stage. He loved them both. And he
would make sure they were safe—or die trying.

Ahead he could see the lights of the cabin. Just ten
days ago he'd seen those lights for the first time.
They'd shone out of the darkness like a beacon from
heaven. And inside he'd found an angel. A sassy
grumpy angel, it was true, but one who'd turned out
to be the woman of his dreams. God help him if he
had to spend the rest of his life only dreaming of her.

Arriving at the outer yard of the property, he circled the perimeter. He saw no vehicle, no guards. He
didn't waste time wondering what that meant. Keeping to the shadows, he crept closer.

THE RUSH SEAT of her ladder-back chair poked
through Shannon's jeans, making her fidget.

Sitting across from her, flipping through a maga-
zine, Larkin looked up. "Sit still." He touched the
gun he'd stuck in his belt and giggled. "Or I'll shoot
you."

Shannon decided not to push her luck. It wasn't
easy, though. Her shoulders hurt from her arms being
pulled back, and her wrists and ankles were chafed
from the rope. But none of it bothered her as much
as her guilt over the things she'd said to Caleb.

Accusing him of being reckless. Insinuating that

their baby deserved better than him as its father. She'd been so unfair. And selfish. She'd give anything to take back her bitter words and tell him how much she respected him.

The past couple of hours had illustrated, as nothing else could, why the world needed people like Caleb and Tony, brave men, honest men, who were willing to put their lives on the line to keep others safe.

Caleb had set out to help rid the world of drugs and the sleazy predators who took advantage of human weakness. And Tony, poor Tony, had just wanted to get the bad guys.

Tony had pushed her away, and in her hurt, she'd let him. She wouldn't make the same mistake with Caleb, she thought. She wouldn't let him forget that he was a human being who needed her as much as she needed him. *I swear if I get out of this alive, I'm going to tell Caleb that I love him. I don't care if he's a cop or a sewer worker.*

A loud noise outside startled her.

Larkin jumped up, gun ready. "What was that?" he whined nervously.

Caleb? *Please, be Caleb.*

"Probably a raccoon," she told him.

He moved to the window over the kitchen sink and looked out. "I don't see anything." He turned back to her. "Are there bears around here?"

She was tempted to tell him that one broke into her cabin last month. But she decided that would only make him more nervous than he already was. And since he had the gun, it didn't seem prudent to upset him. "No, there haven't been bears in this area for generations."

He walked over to the front door and opened it cautiously. "Are you sure?"

There was a scratching sound at the kitchen window. She glanced over and saw Caleb. Her heart stopped, then began to beat wildly.

She looked back at Larkin, who was peering out the front door into the darkness beyond, then returned her gaze to Caleb, hoping against hope that it wasn't her imagination playing tricks on her.

But he was still there, making a sign with his hands. He held up one finger, which she took to mean, *Is Larkin the only one guarding you?*

She nodded slightly.

Then Caleb motioned toward the bathroom.

Instantly she understood and nodded again. "Larkin?"

"What?"

"Could you take these ropes off so I can go to the bathroom?"

He closed the door and moved back to the table. "You just went."

"I know, but I really have to go again." It wasn't easy to smile, since she loathed the man, but for a worthy cause, she managed. "Please?"

"Oh, all right." He squatted down to release her ankles. "But I have to be in there with you." He leered up at her, making her shiver with revulsion.

"I understand," she said, hiding her relief. That was just where she wanted him. Without him in the main room, Caleb could get in unnoticed.

Larkin untied the ropes that held her wrists and stepped back quickly, training the weapon on her.

Shannon stood, her body stiff from sitting in one position so long. She stretched her hands out in front of her, flexing her numb fingers to bring back circulation.

Larkin followed right behind her as she walked slowly to the bathroom. She tried to ignore the fact that a handgun was aimed at the middle of her back and concentrated on getting Larkin out of the way for a few minutes, allowing Caleb to institute his plan.

Once they were both in the bathroom, Larkin shut the door. Shannon's skin crawled to be in such a closed-in space with him.

He looked at her avidly. "I thought you said you had to go."

The guy didn't even have the decency to look away. If for one moment he thought she was going to pull down her jeans and underwear in front of him… "I do, but…you need to turn around." She paused. "Please."

For a moment she thought he was going to refuse, then he turned toward the mirror.

Though she didn't think he'd be able to see her in the mirror, it still gave her the creeps that he tried.

She dawdled as long as she could before Larkin started to get antsy. When she was done, Larkin motioned her to go first. She walked out of the bathroom and it took a great deal of effort not to look around to see where Caleb was lying in wait.

A grunt, followed by the thud of Larkin hitting the floor, answered her question.

Shannon swung around. "Caleb!"

"God, honey, I'm glad to see you." He pulled her to him and gave her a hard kiss, then set her away. "We have to hurry."

An unconscious Larkin lay on his stomach on the floor. Caleb knelt beside him. "Where's Knox?"

Shannon rubbed her arms, trying to keep the fright at bay. "I don't know. He didn't say where he was going."

Caleb took Larkin's gun and stuck it in the back of his jeans, then continued to search him. "Are you all right?" he asked her without looking up.

"Yes, fine." As if she was used to being kidnapped, she thought a little hysterically.

Watching him perform his task in a thorough and professional manner, Shannon felt as if she was watching a totally different man. He looked the same. Ice-blue eyes intense, face tough and compelling. Yet, this was not the Caleb she thought she knew. This one was totally concentrated on his job.

"Get the rope," he ordered.

She walked over to pick the rope off the floor where Larkin had dropped it. The man acted as if rescuing the mother of his baby hadn't fazed him at all, she thought a little resentfully. Would it hurt him to offer a little comfort?

She handed the rope to Caleb.

"Thanks."

"You're welcome." The words sounded stilted to her own ears. What had happened to the vow she'd made while tied up, fearing for her life? Why wasn't she throwing herself into his arms?

She knelt beside him. "Here, let me help you." She secured Larkin's feet, while Caleb took care of his hands.

Caleb looked over at her. "You have any duct tape around here?"

Shannon blinked. "Duct tape? Um, sure." She went into the kitchen and pawed through her junk drawer. Well, what did she expect? Declarations of love?

She brought the tape to him.

He tore off a piece and put it over Larkin's mouth.

Remembering the man's irritating whine, she wished she'd been able to do it sooner.

Caleb stood. He looked her over, as if searching for injury. "Are you well enough to travel?"

His gaze was so cool she wondered if she'd imagined his kiss earlier. The lack of emotion in his eyes made her snap, "I haven't been sick, Agent Carlisle. I was kidnapped."

"I know," he said gruffly. He looked around, his gaze stopping at the coat rack beside the back door. He walked over and grabbed her bulky ski jacket. "Put this on. It's getting cold outside."

Unable to come up with another thing to say in the face of his unsmiling demeanor, she put on the jacket.

She tried to pull up the zipper, but her fingers were shaking so much she couldn't grab hold of the tab.

Caleb pushed her hands aside. "Here, let me do it. We have to get going."

She stood still, fighting to stop reaction to the whole situation from turning her into a quivering mass of Jell-O while Caleb pulled up the zipper, fastened buttons and straightened the collar of the jacket. If he'd been just a fraction gentler, she would have burst into tears. But the anger simmering beneath the surface of his expression kept her stoic.

He picked up a flashlight and walked to the door. "Let's go."

"Where are we going?" she asked as she joined him.

"To find you somewhere safe to stay."

Why was he so angry with her? "Caleb?"

He opened the front door and looked out.

"Caleb, what's wrong?"

He wouldn't look at her.

"Caleb, what did I do?" She hated sounding vulnerable, but after spending so much time longing for him to come for her, she couldn't stand his apparent lack of caring.

His head swung around. "What did *you* do? You didn't do anything." He reached out as if about to touch her, then pulled back his hand. "I don't know how you could even speak to me. It's my fault you were kidnapped."

Her eyes widened. "Your fault?"

"Yes, I trusted the wrong person. But I promise I'll make him pay."

Shannon touched his arm.

He jerked away. "I parked the Jeep down the road. Let's go."

He started down the steps.

Shannon ran after him. "Caleb, wait."

He stopped and turned abruptly to face her. "You don't have to tell me I don't deserve you or our baby. I know it."

God, how could he think she'd hold this against him? "Caleb—"

He put a finger to her lips. "We don't have time to discuss it right now. Knox could show up any minute." He reached for her hand. "Come on."

She went, partly because his grip gave her no choice, partly because she knew that wherever this man went, she would follow. And the first chance she got, she would tell him so.

They kept to the edge of the gravel driveway just

in case they had to take cover in the bushes. Though she was tall, Caleb's legs were longer and she practically had to run to keep up with him.

When she couldn't keep up the pace, she tugged on his hand. "Caleb, slow down a little."

He halted. "Sorry." Then he tightened his grip, and they were on the move again.

An owl flew across the road, startling them both. Shannon let out a nervous laugh.

"Shush!" Caleb ordered.

"Sorry," she said quietly. His reaction made frighteningly clear how perilous their trek was. Just because Knox had driven off in the car didn't mean that he wasn't lying in wait for them. Suddenly the sounds of the night forest she'd always loved took on a sinister quality. Her nerves buzzed at every coo and swish.

They reached the bottom of the road without incident. After that, it was only a few minutes more before they reached the grove of redwood where Caleb had stashed the Jeep.

Shannon leaned against one of the black bumpers to catch her breath. Something struck her as wrong. She looked down. The tire looked low. "God, what else?"

Caleb was at her side. "What's wrong? Are you hurt?"

She pointed at the tire. "Look."

He leaned down to check it out. "It's flat! Damn!" He stood up, then moved to the back of the Jeep and started unfastening the bolt that held the spare. He glanced at her. "Go ahead and sit on that log." He pointed to a felled tree nearby. "I'll take care of it."

It struck Shannon that Caleb took a lot of responsibility on himself. But she was not a helpless flower. "Give me the flashlight. It'll go faster if I help."

"All right." He handed it to her. "But stand out of the way. I don't need you getting hurt."

"Thanks for the vote of confidence." She turned on the light and shone it at the car—and the bottom dropped out of her stomach.

"Caleb?" she said quietly.

In the process of getting out the jack, he glanced back. "What?"

Shannon swallowed roughly. "I don't have enough spares to change all four."

Chapter Fourteen

Caleb circled the Jeep. All four tires were flat.

So, Knox knew he was here.

Caleb pulled out his weapon and opened his mouth to caution Shannon.

A shot rang out, splintering tree bark inches above his head.

He grabbed Shannon's arm and pulled her down behind the disabled vehicle. "Get down! Damn! I'd hoped we'd have more time."

"If it's Knox, why didn't we see his car?" Shannon whispered from beside him.

"Because he's playing games," Caleb told her. He didn't know why it had taken him so long to figure this out. Knox was a game player. Act like you're a great cop, blow away the competition. Kidnap the key witness. Leave her virtually unattended.

Knox had never expected Caleb to go after the money first.

"Carlisle!"

Knox's call sounded from the cover of trees across the road.

"What do you want?" Caleb called back to him.

"What I always wanted—the money."

"You've made the Jeep undrivable. How am I supposed to go looking for it now?"

"I'm sure you'll think of something. You have one hour, or I give the orders to kill Munoz's wife and kids."

Shannon drew in a shocked breath. Caleb put a hand on her arm and gave a little squeeze.

"One hour, Carlisle."

An engine started, and they heard a car drive off. Caleb stood and helped Shannon up beside him.

"What money?" she asked.

"The money from the drug deal we were supposed to be doing with the Driscoes. At the hospital Brandon told me that before he was shot he'd gone back to the compound to retrieve the backpacks we'd used to transport the cash. He hid them."

"Why didn't Knox just go find them himself?"

"Because it's not part of the game," Caleb told her grimly. He took his cell phone out of his pocket and dialed the captain's direct number.

"Gallagher."

"It's Carlisle. I'm down the road from Shannon's place," Caleb said into the phone. "She's safe. I've got Larkin secured. But there's a problem. Knox is going after Munoz's wife and kids now. It'll take him at least forty minutes to get there—"

"He already has them."

Caleb's stomach knotted. "What? How?" If he hurt that family…

"Carlos Morales." The captain didn't need to say more.

Suddenly it all came together for Caleb. All the hints, all the doubts. The knots in his stomach tightened. He had to think fast to keep up the pretense. "Morales? Are you sure?"

"Afraid so."

"But he's Munoz's wife's cousin. How could he do this to his own family?"

"He's a drug addict, Carlisle. That's why he had to resign from the SDU. Why would you expect anything else?"

Why, indeed? Caleb thought. Maybe because like every other citizen he expected the people who'd signed on to protect them to be trustworthy. Especially when it was the man he'd taken orders from for twelve years.

Carlos Morales wasn't the bad guy here. Gallagher was. Caleb knew firsthand how Carlos had struggled to get on the straight and narrow, to repair the damage he'd done to his life. He'd never get involved in a drug-dealing scheme. Unlike, apparently, Captain Sean Gallagher.

But Caleb couldn't let on to the captain what he'd suddenly pieced together.

"Then I'd better go get that money," he told the captain, who said he'd keep working on things on his end.

"You do that."

Caleb hung up and looked at Shannon.

"An hour, Caleb. Can we do it?"

He put his arm around her and pulled her to him. She responded by laying her head on his chest and hugging him tightly.

He kissed her on the forehead. "We can do it, honey. We have to."

"So let's go."

He hesitated. Her pregnancy hadn't been far from

his mind all day. The terrain was treacherous in broad
daylight. At night, even with a full moon, it could be
deadly. And that was without factoring in a crazy man
with a weapon. "It's a couple of miles. I'm not sure
you should be hiking that distance in your condition."

"I'll be fine. Besides, we don't have to walk."

He raised a brow. "We don't?"

"Well, only just up the driveway. I have a truck in
the garage."

"You have a truck in the garage," Caleb repeated
evenly. "You never mentioned any truck last week
when I was worried about leaving you with no transportation."

"I know." Shannon shrugged. "You were in no
shape to drive. If I'd told you I had an automatic four-
wheel-drive truck, you would have insisted on taking
it. And ended up in some ditch," she said stubbornly.

Well, that was probably the truth, but that didn't
explain— "Why the hell didn't you tell me about it
back at the cabin?"

"I...In my fear, I forgot about it."

She looked so miserable that Caleb felt like a heel.
After all she'd been through, it wasn't fair of him to
expect her to think calmly.

"Let's go." He took her hand and they walked
back up the driveway. "Do you know where the keys
are?"

"They're in the pickup," she said softly.

Five minutes later they were in Shannon's four-
wheel-drive three-quarter-ton pickup, heading down
the mountain.

Caleb reached over and squeezed her hand. "I'm
sorry."

She cleared her throat. "I'm sorry, too. I should have thought—"

"You were terrified. It's not your fault." It was his, for getting her in this situation in the first place. He wondered if he'd ever have a chance to make it up to her.

Between the truck's powerful engine and the lack of traffic, Caleb was able to cut the trip to the compound's entrance by half. After bouncing around for another ten minutes, they arrived at their destination.

Caleb parked, pocketed the keys and walked around to meet Shannon on the other side. "Brandon was pretty sure he'd gone this way after he grabbed the bags."

He took her hand and pulled her along with him. He drew his weapon just in case Knox decided to show up.

A fox ran across their path, making them both jump. The wind blew up again, chilling the air.

"How could Brandon remember one hollowed-out tree trunk when there are so many?" Shannon asked.

"He has a good eye for details." What he hadn't known was where that tree was.

An owl hooted, startling him. His hand went to his weapon. He wouldn't put it past Knox to be out there playing his games.

The night forest was full of strange sounds. By the time they reached a clearing, he'd almost blown away two owls and a raccoon.

Shannon stopped and sat on a fallen log. "I'm sorry. I need to rest for a moment. My legs are killing me."

Caleb sat next to her. "I've been pushing you awfully hard. I'm sorry."

Shannon shook her head. "If you apologize one more time, I'm going to hit you. This isn't your fault. You are not responsible for Knox's crimes."

"I know that," Caleb said. He reached for her hand, but kept his gaze moving, ever watchful.

Shannon stood. "All right, I'm ready again."

Caleb rose to stand beside her. "Are you sure?"

"Which way?" She looked up at him expectantly.

He didn't know. Brandon couldn't tell him. Caleb looked around, trying to put himself in his partner's shoes. "Let's try this way."

They tromped the dew-ridden ferns, legs aching, eyes on the lookout for something, anything that looked as though it might be the hiding place for a quarter of a million dollars.

Shannon never asked to rest again, and Caleb's love and respect for her grew by leaps and bounds. Where had she gotten such determination, such grit?

Just when he thought his sprained ankle couldn't hold him a minute longer, Shannon stopped and pointed. "Could that be it?"

He eyed the burned-out tree trunk. It seemed to fit Brandon's description. Unfortunately, it was taller than he'd thought it might be. "If it is, we're going to need a ladder." He holstered his gun.

She walked over to the tree. "No, you don't. You can give me a boost. I'll shine the flashlight inside."

He joined her. "I'm not going to put you at risk."

"Come on, Caleb. I climbed plenty of trees in my childhood. This'll be easy."

He touched her cheek. "You weren't carrying my baby then."

She held his hand to her face. "Caleb, think of

Agent Munoz's family. If the captain can't get to them, it's up to us to save them.''

"Shannon, Marissa and the kids aren't going to be hurt. Trust me on this.''

"I do trust you, Caleb. But trust goes both ways. I can do this. You have to let me help.''

She was right. He knew it. Even if Sid's family survived unharmed, there were others. Who knew where Knox would strike next?

They had no choice.

But to put his own family in jeopardy...

Shannon kissed his cheek. "We have no choice.''

Because she was right, Caleb gave in.

Bracing his leg, he held her hand while she used him as a step. She turned on the flashlight and looked over the edge of the trunk. "They're here.''

She grabbed the two backpacks. "Now help me get down.''

"Yes, Carlisle, help the lady down.''

Knox. He'd set the trap—and Caleb had walked right into it.

Caleb got Shannon safely to the ground and took the packs from her. There was no way he could reach his gun in time.

"Turn around and drop the bags,'' Knox ordered.

Caleb turned, then took the necessary step to put himself in front of Shannon, blocking her body. For what it was worth. One bullet could take them both. "You just keep showing up, don't you?''

Knox smiled. "That was a nice move. Step out, Ms. Garrett, or I'll kill him right now.''

Shannon did as he ordered.

He aimed his gun at Shannon. "Give me the packs, Carlisle.''

Caleb had a feeling of déjà vu.

Inching toward Shannon, he tried to calculate the distance between him and Knox. Could he hit the other man with one of the packs? Or at least distract him?

He felt Shannon touch his back.

"Get behind me, honey," he whispered.

Knox laughed. "Isn't that touching? You're going to sacrifice yourself for her. Has it occurred to you that once I've shot you, she'll be defenseless?"

It had occurred to him. "You're low, Knox. But a cop killer? You'd better resign yourself to life on the run, 'cause there'll be nowhere deep enough for you to hide."

Suddenly he realized that Shannon's hand had gone under his jacket. He felt cold steel against the skin of his back. She was going for Larkin's gun!

Damn! What did she think she was doing?

"You're right," Knox said as he took a couple of steps closer.

His voice was cool and devoid of emotion, but Caleb sensed an undercurrent of tension.

"Maybe I don't want to kill you. Or maybe I have no choice."

Caleb glared at him. "What the hell does that mean?"

"It means that thanks to the Driscoe brothers, I owe some very scary men a lot of money. A hint of betrayal will get a man's throat slit."

Caleb stiffened as Shannon slipped the weapon out of his pants, sending chills down his back. "So I give you the money, Knox. Then what?"

"Well, you got me there, buddy. I can't exactly let you two run around gathering the troops, can I?"

No, he couldn't, Caleb thought. Which meant if he and Shannon were going to get out of this alive, he had to come up with a plan fast.

"Give me the bags." Knox shook the gun as if to remind them he had a deadly weapon trained on them.

Shannon stepped back, pulling Caleb with her.

Since she now had the gun in her hand, he had to keep in front of her. His mind was going a mile a minute.

Without moving his gaze from Knox, he whispered to Shannon, "Get ready to run."

She squeezed his arm, signaling her agreement.

As Knox approached them, Caleb swung the bags at his outstretched hand, the one that held the gun. Then he shouted, "Now!"

Shannon took off into the trees, and Caleb followed, clearly registering Knox's bellow of rage.

"Keep going straight ahead, honey. I'm right behind you."

His own gun in one hand, the bags in the other, Caleb kept his eye on Shannon while listening for the sound of Knox behind them. The wind whipped her hair back as she ran, agilely avoiding ferns and branches.

He heard Knox cursing in the distance. They'd gotten a good head start on him.

He caught up to Shannon. "Are you okay? Do you want to stop for a minute?"

"Don't be ridiculous!" she snapped.

The sound of rushing water reached his ears. "There's a stream not too far ahead. We'll have to cross to the other side to avoid the mudslide."

"Okay."

There was that grit again, Caleb thought. A lot of

people would have fallen apart when faced with a gun. Which reminded him. "Let me see your gun."

She handed it to him. "*My* gun?"

"It is now," he told her, checking to make sure the safety was on.

He handed it back to her. "Use it if you have to."

Pushing aside some bushes, they continued their trek. "The stream's just ahead."

"Carlisle!" Knox's shout sounded quite a distance away, but it was still too close for comfort.

A shot rang out. Then another.

Ahead, the river raced over smooth rocks, deep, black and menacing in the moonlight.

"It's too deep here," Shannon said. "I know a better crossing upstream."

Caleb followed her directions. This was her territory, after all.

They traveled alongside the water for a while, coming to a stop on a sandy landing to catch their breath. Then he pushed her gently. "Go on. I'll follow."

She kept moving, keeping an eye out for a safe place to cross.

Caleb touched her arm. "Look, just ahead. See those boulders in the water?"

"I see them."

"Do you think you can negotiate those?"

"Sure," she said as she reached the spot. "I spent half my childhood bouncing over boulders like that."

He grinned. "First trees, now rocks. What other surprises do you have in store for me?"

She smiled, quoting his own words back to him. "I'll explain later."

"I'll remind you." There was a husky tinge to his voice that struck an answering note in her. The man was as potent as whiskey. He went straight to her head. Which was probably not the best reaction to have when you were on the run from a gun-toting drug-dealing piece of scum.

She stepped onto the first boulder.

"Careful."

"Don't worry," she told him. Easy to say, she thought as she tried to get her footing. She put her arms out for balance and stepped onto the next boulder. Only a few more feet and she'd be across.

A shot rang out.

"Go, Shannon!" Caleb yelled.

Knowing that to be careful now would only put her in jeopardy, Shannon jumped from one stone to the next, trusting her old agility to keep her from falling.

Another shot rang out as she landed on muddy but solid land. She took refuge behind a huge redwood. Immediately she pulled the gun out of her jacket pocket, where she'd placed it as she'd crossed the river. Releasing the safety, she searched for a sign of Caleb.

She saw him just as he slipped on a wet boulder.

She held her breath, afraid that calling out would bring him to Knox's attention. "Come on, come on," she urged under her breath.

She heard the next shot hit the water inches in front of Caleb.

She took aim and fired across the stream.

Caleb took two rocks at a time, dived onto the bank and rolled into the nearby bushes. "Shannon, put that thing away!"

She fired again. "No."

"I don't want you getting hurt."

She took aim. "Neither did Tony. That's why he

insisted I take courses in shooting handguns and rifles.''

"He what?"

She focused on Knox. "You heard me."

A shot splintered a branch above her, sending needles raining down.

She and Caleb returned fire.

He fired off a couple of rounds, then crawled over to join her behind the tree. "Why didn't you tell me?"

"A girl's gotta have some secrets," she said, attempting to sound sultry and mysterious.

He pulled her close and covered her mouth with his. The kiss was hot, intense and way too short. "Not from me, ever again."

"Carlisle, give it up," Knox called out. "You don't have enough ammunition to hold out against me. Give me the money, and I'll give the order to let Munoz and the kids go. Otherwise..."

He didn't finish his statement, leaving it to their imagination.

Shannon gripped Caleb's arm. "We can take care of ourselves, but those babies..." God, she couldn't stand the idea of someone hurting those little kids. "The money isn't important."

"Honey," Caleb said, "I told you that Marissa and the kids will be fine." He could see she wanted desperately to believe him, but there was still doubt in her eyes.

"Shannon, this man is responsible for taking too many lives. I have to end this now."

She gripped his arm. "What about Captain Gallagher? Can you contact him?"

He took out his cell phone, flipped it open and pressed in the number.

Gallagher answered, his tone official.

Anger-driven bile rose to Caleb's throat. He fought it, knowing he couldn't afford to let on what he knew.

"It's Carlisle," he said quietly, successfully hiding his disgust. "Have you found Marissa and the kids?"

"Yeah, they're at Morales's house. I have men staked out there."

Caleb's mouth tightened. Yeah, but which men? he thought.

"Have you talked to Morales?"

"He says he'll let them go once you give Knox the money. Otherwise, he'll kill them. You have to do what they want, Carlisle."

You mean what you *want, Captain,* Caleb thought.

"Carlisle?"

"Yeah, Captain?"

"Don't do anything stupid."

"No, I won't do that," Caleb said. It should be easier now that he knew exactly who he was up against.

Trust yourself, Gallagher had told him earlier. As if he had a choice. There was no one else to trust.

"One more thing, Carlisle."

"What?"

"I'm sending a couple of men out to the compound. Head back there. It's your only chance."

"Right, we'll meet you there," Caleb said quietly though it took everything in him not to rage at the man who'd betrayed everything Caleb thought he'd stood for. The man who'd lied through his teeth.

If Caleb was stupid enough to head for the compound, he knew he wouldn't find the salvation Sean Gallagher had promised.

He heard a plopping sound, like a fish jumping in water. Shannon tugged Caleb's sleeve and pointed. He looked toward the stream and saw Knox making his way across.

Caleb got off a shot, placing it just in front of Knox's feet. "Freeze, Knox, or you're dead where you stand."

Knox squeezed off a shot and dove behind a huge boulder. The bullet hit a tree, landing just inches above their heads.

Keeping his gaze on the boulder, Caleb put his phone away. "Shannon, are you really as good with that gun as you claim?"

"Yes. What do you want me to do?"

He didn't want her to have to do anything, but he had no choice if she was to be safe. "Your cabin isn't that far from here. That's where we're heading." The lie almost choked him. She'd be furious when she realized he hadn't followed.

"Knox will follow us," she said.

"Not right away. I'm going to hold him off here," Caleb told her.

"I won't leave without you," she said stubbornly.

"Yes, you will," he said harshly, never taking his gaze from the boulder Knox hid behind. It shamed him that Shannon would be safer at the cabin with Larkin trussed up like a pig, than at the compound with his fellow agents.

"But first, I want you to cover me so I can get in a better position. Aim at the rocks in front of Knox without hitting him. Can you do that?"

She took a deep breath. "Yes," she whispered, "but I don't have many rounds left."

"Your few shots will keep Knox behind that boulder," Caleb told her. "That's all I need. Understand?"

"Yes, I understand."

"Good, I'll count to three. You shoot and then take off that way. I'll take over from there. You run and keep on running. Ready?"

"No."

He glanced at her. "No?" His peripheral vision caught movement from the stream. He squeezed off a shot. "Don't even think about it, Knox," he yelled out, then lowered his voice. "What do you mean, no?"

"I'm not leaving, Caleb. That's the stupidest idea I've ever heard. And you're not a stupid man."

Caleb was speechless. At no point did he expect her to refuse to go along with his plan.

"Tell me what's going on, Caleb. The truth."

Caleb thought of telling her, but decided she would be safer not knowing. "Listen, honey, this is our best chance to get ahead of this guy. I have to get close enough to get the drop on him. This is the way it has to be. Now do what I say."

The command in his voice brooked no defiance. Though Shannon wanted to argue more, she knew that she had to trust Caleb to know what he was doing. She only wished she could be sure he wasn't sacrificing himself for her and the baby.

"Do it now, Shannon. I'll follow as soon as I can."

Fear clutching at her stomach, Shannon took careful aim at the boulders three feet in front of Knox. "Ready."

"One, two, *three!*"

She emptied the cartridge, then turned and ran. The terrain steepened as she moved. She knew this area. Her own property was just ahead.

She thought of the night Caleb had shown up at her cabin. He'd climbed this same hill, bleeding and injured. It still amazed her that he'd made it *this* far, much less all the way to her cabin.

Her legs began to ache from the climb, and the sound of her breathing was so loud she couldn't hear Caleb crashing through the undergrowth behind her. So she looked behind to check, and didn't see him. Still moving, she held her breath a moment, trying to hear. Nothing. Only the pounding of her heart.

She stopped and turned abruptly. Caleb hadn't followed. He'd never planned to. He'd stayed behind to take on Knox himself.

Alone.

The very word wreaked havoc in her heart. He'd stayed behind to fight Knox alone.

The reality rocked her. And she knew what she had to do. She started back down the hill.

Her man was in trouble. There was no way she was going to sit around waiting for news like a good girl. She'd already done that once—and she hadn't liked the news they'd brought her. This time she was making sure things turned out differently.

Chapter Fifteen

While Shannon escaped, Caleb kept Knox pinned behind the boulder. Whenever Knox dared to move, Caleb squeezed off a shot.

"You can't keep this up forever, Carlisle," Knox taunted.

"The extra clips in my pocket tell me otherwise." Actually he only had one extra clip, but Knox didn't—and wouldn't—know that. Once Shannon realized he wasn't following, she would go to her cabin and phone for help. Reinforcements would arrive and finally Knox would be arrested.

"And when those run out?" Knox laughed. "Or are you planning to kill me before that happens?"

Caleb gritted his teeth. "Why not? You put a bullet in my partner's back."

Knox laughed. "You're too goody-goody to kill a man in cold blood. Everything you do is by the book."

"You could be wrong. I thought the same about you once."

"Well, you know how it is, things come up. Everly shouldn't have taken my money."

"Money," Caleb spit out. "Twenty years as a cop, and you'd kill a fellow officer for money?"

Let the scum think he was surprised by his motives. If he thought Caleb was that dumb, he might be lulled into making a move.

"Don't be naive, Carlisle. As cops we make barely a living wage while the drug traffickers live in mansions and drive around in luxury cars. Can you honestly tell me it hasn't occurred to you that they have the better deal?"

Caleb didn't bother to answer. Instead, he concentrated on the barely perceptible movements Knox had been making as he talked. The light of the moon allowed him to see Knox's reflection in the stream. He'd moved back from the rock, edging toward the far bank. Probably figuring to lose himself in the forest.

"Stop right there, Knox!"

He didn't wait for the man to obey. He shot. The bullet hit inches from Knox's feet. Knox jumped back, lost his footing and fell into the rushing stream.

Caleb threw the money sacks behind a boulder, shoved his gun into his waistband and took off over the damp rocks into the stream. In seconds he reached the point where Knox floundered in the water and fished him out.

Knox took a swing at him. Caleb deflected it with his left forearm and made a jab with his right. His fist caught Knox's jaw, and the man went down. Grabbing Knox's wet jacket, Caleb pulled him up and hit him again. Without giving him time to react, he grasped Knox's jacket and started dragging him toward the bank. He threw the groaning Knox facedown on the damp earth. Holding him down with a knee in his back, he unfastened his leather belt. It wasn't the best substitute for handcuffs, but it would do.

"Malcolm Knox, you're under arrest for—"

"Let him go, Carlisle." At the sound of the familiar voice, Caleb looked up. Captain Gallagher stood just a few feet away, weapon drawn and aimed at him. "And drop your piece."

Caleb hung his head for a moment, pulled his gun from his waistband and dropped it to the muddy ground. He stood away from Knox. "So I was right."

Knox sat up with a groan. "It's about time you got here." Blood trickled slowly from a cut on his forehead. He touched a hand to it. "I hit my head on one of those damned rocks."

"You'll survive," Caleb sneered. "The devil takes care of his own."

Then, unable to stand the sight of the man, he focused his attention on Gallagher. Disgust, anger and sadness warred within him.

"I didn't want to believe it," he said bitterly. "Even when I knew deep down it was true, I didn't want to believe that you could stoop so low. Why?"

The older man—his captain, the man he'd trusted for twelve years—said nothing.

"Dammit, answer me!" he cried. "You were a good man, a good cop. What turned you? Was the money that important? How could you do this to your daughter?"

Always a big man, Gallagher seemed to shrink before Caleb's eyes.

Knox heaved himself off the ground. "Why are you wasting time listening to his blabber, Gallagher? Kill him and let's go find the money."

"Stop right there, gentlemen," a new voice ordered.

Caleb's heart stopped. Several feet behind Gallagher stood Shannon with her gun aimed at the two men. Her empty gun, dammit!

Knox laughed. "And how do you propose to shoot us, Miss Know-It-All, with no bullets?"

"What makes you think I have no bullets?" she asked with amazing confidence.

The minute they got out of this mess, he was going to kiss her senseless, Caleb thought. Then give her a sound telling-off for taking such a stupid chance. She was supposed to be off calling for help, not riding back in like the bloody cavalry to save him!

"Sound carries in the forest," Knox informed her. "I heard your conversation with Carlisle."

She raised an eyebrow. "And you believe I'd actually be dumb enough to empty my gun?" she asked haughtily. "And go off into the forest with no protection whatsoever? When there was a chance I'd run into some snake in the grass like your captain here?"

Caleb glanced at the captain. The older man had such a look of shame on his face he almost felt sorry for him. Instead, he took the steps necessary to relieve the man of his weapon.

"Noooo!" Knox yelled.

The next thing Caleb knew he was hit by a flying tackle and knocked to the ground so hard the breath was pounded out of him. Knox grabbed for his gun, but Caleb held on to it tightly as he hit out at Knox.

Knox punched at him again and again, then made another attempt to grab the weapon. They rolled over the wet rocky ground. Suddenly Knox's hand closed over his and squeezed. There was a loud bang as the gun went off.

Shannon screamed.

Caleb gathered every bit of strength he had left and threw a punch at Knox's jaw, knocking him out. His breath rasped harshly as he climbed to his feet. He looked around wildly until his gaze found Shannon.

She was on her knees a few feet away. Next to her lay the captain.

He limped over to her and touched her shoulder. "Shannon, are you all right?"

She looked up. "I'm fine. When the gun went off, he went down. He's hit and he's bleeding pretty badly." Suddenly her eyes widened and she gasped, "Caleb, behind you!"

Caleb turned to see Knox just a few feet away, a branch held like a club in his hand. With a grunt he swung it down.

Caleb raised his left arm to deflect the blow, but the branch made contact.

Pain shot from his arm to his shoulder and drove him to his knees.

"You've ruined everything, Carlisle," he heard Knox growl through the haze of pain. "I'll kill you if it's the last thing I do." Knox raised the branch, then swung with deadly intent.

Caleb threw himself to the side, covering his head with his good arm.

Then he heard a shot.

With a look of amazement, Knox crumpled to the ground and lay still. A blossom of red flowered on his shoulder.

Shannon ran up to him. "Caleb, are you all right?"

"Is Knox dead?" He struggled up.

"I think so," she said, helping him to stand. "He's not moving. Forget him. What about you?"

"Arm's broken, but I'll live." He leaned down and gave her a brief hard kiss. "Thank God you're a terrific shot."

"I didn't shoot him," she said. "I was bluffing, Caleb. My gun *was* empty."

"Then who…?"

Caleb looked over at the captain, who sat on the ground, leaning against a tree. His face looked deathly pale in the moonlight.

"I couldn't let him kill you." The smoking gun fell from his hand.

Cradling his injured arm and grateful for Shannon's steady arm behind his back, Caleb limped over to Gallagher.

"It was gambling. I owed so much money." He coughed, then groaned, clutching his side.

Caleb knelt beside the man who'd been like a father to him for twelve years. Anger boiled up inside him. "How deep in debt were you, you bastard? How many people died because of you and Knox?"

The older man shook his head. "Have to explain… Threatened to k-kill my daughter…failed her for so long…couldn't let them hurt her."

He paused. "Couldn't let them hurt a good man."

"What about Brandon? He's a good man, too. They shot him in the back!"

Gallagher shook his head. "Didn't know… Knox told me you'd shot him by accident." He took a deep breath. "He said you killed the Driscoes. Only later…found out the truth…" He closed his eyes and slumped over.

Caleb shook him. "Wake up, dammit! You're not going to die on me now."

"He's passed out," Shannon said gently. She picked up Gallagher's wrist and checked for a pulse, her expression grave. "It's weak. We need to get him help now." She reached out and touched Caleb's arm, and tears sprang to her eyes. "We need to get you both help."

Caleb tried to stand. His head swam and he fought not to pass out. It was his job to take care of Shannon.

"Caleb?"

He tried to focus on her lovely face, but his vision was blurred.

"Caleb, don't faint on me! Not out here."

"I won't." He reached for her, felt her hand. Pain shot through him. A swarm of angry bees buzzed inside his head. He wanted to tell her something, had to tell her.

"The baby..." He started to speak, but a black hole opened in front of his eyes, threatening to swallow him. "Sorry...ruined everything." He fell into the black hole.

Shannon caught Caleb as he keeled over. "Dammit, Caleb, don't do this."

She wanted to sob as she eased him to the ground. She couldn't lose him, not now. She felt his pulse. It was strong and steady. The physical beatings he'd taken over the past week had probably just been too much for his body to take.

She pushed back his jacket, took his cell phone off his belt and dialed 911. When the dispatcher answered, she explained the circumstances and gave directions.

Keeping her eyes on Caleb, she leaned against a

tree and waited, trying hard not to react to his statement. Did he really think the baby had ruined everything? If so, she thought, then it was time to get out of his life.

She looked down at the man who had come into her life only ten days ago. Moonlight shone through the branches, casting a glow on his tough form. Even battered and bruised, he had the most compelling face she'd ever seen. She reached out to touch him, running a finger down his cheek, longing for him to flash those sexy dimples of his.

She'd spent three long years in her lonely tower of a cabin, exiled from life by her grief. Tony's death and the loss of their baby had been so devastating that she'd pulled away from everyone and everything. And she'd probably still be there, thinking she was perfectly content, if Caleb hadn't stumbled onto her porch.

She reached down and stroked back his damp hair. "But you did, Caleb Carlisle," she said aloud, wanting him to hear. "You came into my life, you looked at me and brought every emotion I'd tried to kill back to life."

She reached for his limp hand and held it tightly.

"You made love to me in a way I never dreamed possible," she said more gently. "And now we're having a baby. So if you think you can just walk away, you'd better think again. I'll fight for you with everything in me to give us and our baby the family we deserve."

She heard a sound, turned to look and suddenly she was being hauled to her feet.

"How touching," Knox sneered, pushing the barrel of his gun into her ribs.

"I thought you were dead," she said.

"And I thought you were smart. Which just goes to prove we can both be wrong." He shoved her forward. "Let's go."

His fingers dug into her upper arm as he forced her up the hill. Shannon's mind raced as she tried to figure a way out of this one. She could throw her weight against him; surely his injuries had weakened him. It would be fairly easy to make him fall, but there was still no guarantee he wouldn't fire at her before she could get away. And if she did get away, would he come after her or go straight back to Caleb, who was lying defenseless on the ground?

No, she'd just have to go with him for now. "Where are we going?"

"Your place to get Larkin. Then I come back to find the money."

She stumbled over a branch. "Watch it." He hauled her up before she could fall.

His breath sounded harsh in her ear. The loss of blood and strenuous activity were taking their toll. Maybe if she could keep him talking, make him think it wasn't safe… "I called 911. The police are on their way."

He laughed. "I'll be long gone by the time those clowns figure out where you are. Too bad I won't be there to see the look on Carlisle's face when he finds you dead in that little cabin where you saved his life last week."

Shannon shuddered at the image. "You're mad."

"No, just smart," Knox said, the arrogance in his voice losing power as he started coughing.

He was getting weaker. She just might have a chance here.

"But Larkin won't be there," she taunted.

"Oh, he'll be there," Knox said hoarsely. "Unless the two of you killed him. And Carlisle is too much of a goody-goody to do that. No, Larkin is just where you left him. He'll be damn grateful I'm there to rescue him."

Shannon saw the lights of her cabin in the distance. Dread filled her. She might have been able to take an exhausted injured Knox alone, but if Larkin had really been lying there tied up all this time, he was going to be out for blood.

SOMEONE SLAPPED him. "Caleb, Caleb, wake up!"

Caleb opened his eyes and tried to focus on the face above him. "Sid?"

"Yeah, it's me." His arm went around Caleb's back. "You need to sit up."

Caleb let Sid help him into a sitting position. Pain streaked through his injured arm and he groaned.

"Your arm broke?"

"Yeah," Caleb gritted out.

"Medic, over here."

A paramedic set down a large case and knelt beside him. "Tell me your injuries."

"Broken arm, I think. That's the worst of it." The scrapes and bruises were negligible.

As the paramedic felt his arm, Caleb looked at Sid. "Did Shannon tell you about the captain?"

Sid's expression was grave. "Caleb, Shannon's not here."

"I'm going to put a sling on your arm to restrain movement," the paramedic said.

"Whatever," Caleb snapped, not taking his gaze off the other agent. "What do you mean, Shannon's not here? Where did she go? She left the three of us and went off on her own?''

"Not three,'' Sid said. "Two. You and the captain.''

The bottom dropped out of Caleb's world. "Where's Knox?'' He looked around. "He was the mastermind of all this. Where is he?'' he was yelling now.

"Sir, you'll have to calm down,'' the paramedic interjected. "Your arm is in need of attention.''

Caleb knew there was no way he was going to be able to walk with his broken arm dangling helplessly at his side. He glared at the paramedic. "Okay. Secure that thing.''

He seethed as the paramedic, working quickly and efficiently, wrapped his left arm in a sling. Then he looked at Sid.

"Help me up,'' he ordered with supreme calm. "Knox must have taken Shannon as a hostage. We're going to get her back.''

"Caleb, you're in no shape—''

"I'm not asking you for permission, Munoz.''

Sid helped him to stand.

"I need a weapon. Give me your extra.''

Sid reached into his coat and brought out his extra gun, which he handed to Caleb. "You need to see a doctor. You can't be running around this forest—''

Caleb cut him off. "Knox has been screwing with this agency way too long. He has my woman, and I'm going after her. You can stay here and baby-sit that bastard''—he glanced at the still-unconscious captain, who was being tended by the paramedics—"or you can come with me. It's your choice.''

Sid stared into his eyes for a moment, then nodded. "I'm with you."

Two more agents burst through the trees. "Hey, Carlisle, couldn't you have had a showdown somewhere closer to town?" Agent Scatini asked.

"You want a showdown, come with us," Caleb said.

He headed into the woods, not bothering to see if the others had followed. Knox was the ultimate game player. You didn't leave the board till the game was done. It would be just like him to take Shannon back to her cabin. Because Caleb would know where to look.

BY THE TIME Shannon and Knox reached the cabin, he was breathing harshly. It was clear the climb had taken its toll, but not once had he eased his grip on her arm or his gun. She might have admired his determination and resiliency if she wasn't so scared.

He pushed her up the steps. "Open it."

She obeyed, and he shoved her inside, kicking the door shut behind him.

Larkin lay bound and gagged, bloodshot eyes open and furious.

Knox aimed his weapon at her. "Untie him."

Unable to think of a way out of it, she walked over and knelt at Larkin's feet, then began to work with shaking hands on the intricate knots Caleb had made. One piece she pulled on just made the knots tighter. The man knew how to tie a rope, that was for sure.

Larkin tried to talk through his gag.

"Shut up," Knox ordered. "You got yourself into this mess."

Shannon was glad Knox hadn't ordered her to take

off the gag first. She couldn't have stood to hear Larkin's screechy voice when her nerves were already stretched to the limit.

"Hurry up!" Knox ordered.

"I'm trying," she said. She looked up at him and noticed he seemed to be swaying on his feet. Though his expression was livid, his face was as pale as a ghost. Shifting her gaze to the wound high on his chest, she noticed that the bloodstain seemed to be getting bigger.

He brandished his weapon. "Damn you, I said hurry!"

She returned to her task, a plan forming. The longer she took to unfasten the ropes, the longer he would have to stand over her. He'd already lost a lot of blood. If she could stall long enough, he might just end up passing out.

The only problem was, Knox was a smart man. He'd be able to tell if she wasn't really trying. She had to make her incompetence believable. But how?

"Get those ropes undone or I'll kill you now!" he screamed. He stomped his foot on the floor.

She flinched involuntarily. And suddenly she knew what she had to do.

She made her hands fumble on the ropes and started to cry. "I'm trying!" she sobbed. "Please stop yelling at me. You're making me nervous."

"If you don't want me to yell, then get those ropes off."

She released an end, to prove she was trying. "I will. Just don't hurt me."

"Don't hurt you? You haven't begun to feel how much I can hurt you. You and your boyfriend have ruined everything. This was going to be the last shipment I arranged. The powers that be were getting greedy. I told them it was getting iffy, that they needed to move on. But did they listen to me?''

They might not have, Shannon thought, but she was listening to every single word. The man was spilling his guts. And she was going to remember everything he said.

''No, they didn't listen to me,'' Knox rambled on. ''They knew best. Even when I told them I'd gotten wind of this undercover operation, they didn't care. Just get us the money, they said. Show me the money, like that stupid football player in that movie.''

Shannon watched out of the corner of her eye as he moved restlessly. The blood loss must be making him light-headed. He probably didn't know what he was saying. But he still had the gun, so she kept working on the ropes.

''Well, I'll show them the money. That 250 grand is marked. As soon as those jerks spend it, they'll be marked, too. And I'll be free.''

So that was why those backpacks of cash were so important to him, Shannon thought. He didn't want the money for himself. He needed it to set up his bosses.

''Aren't you done yet? You incompetent bitch, can't you do anything?'' He shoved her out of the way and grasped the end of the rope with his free hand. ''Do I have to do everything myself?''

She rolled away from him toward the kitchen table and up onto her feet.

Just then the front door burst open, and two shots rang out.

Knox fell to the floor.

''Shannon, get away from him!''

She swung around. "Caleb!"

He stood, gun pointed at Knox, who lay bleeding from his wounds.

"Go ahead, Carlisle," Knox rasped. "Finish me off."

Caleb shook his head. "Too easy, Knox. I want you to serve out every second of your long sentence."

Three men piled into the room, weapons drawn. They swarmed around Knox and Larkin.

Shannon barely noticed. All she could see was all she wanted.

Caleb Carlisle, cop.

He holstered his weapon and held out his good arm. Shannon ran to him, her arms circling his waist, holding on for dear life.

He grunted and she jumped back. "I'm sorry. I hurt you."

"I don't care." He pulled her back against him. "Come here."

And then he brought his mouth down on hers. She met his kiss with every bit of passion within her.

Again and again they kissed, until they were both breathless.

He cupped her face. "I love you, Shannon. When I found out he'd taken you again, I thought I'd die. I don't ever want you out of my sight again. Do you hear me?"

She laughed. "I hear you."

And then she stared into his gorgeous sky-blue eyes. "I love you, too. When you said the baby had ruined everything, it hurt so much. But I know once you get used to the idea—"

"Shh." He put a finger on her lips. "I *want* the baby. I *want* you. I didn't mean the baby had ruined everything. I was trying to apologize for bringing you into this mess.''

She kissed his finger. ''It wasn't your fault.''

He smiled, flashing that wonderful dimple. ''It doesn't matter. We're all safe now. And you and I are going to make a wonderful home for our child.'' His gaze caught hers.

She read it all there in his eyes.

''It's everything I've ever wanted, Shannon. A beautiful wife, a terrific child, a family. Will you marry me?''

Shannon's heart swelled with love. For Caleb. For their baby. ''Oh, yes.''

Epilogue

Shannon stood on the balcony of Caleb's condo in Santa Cruz. Though they'd spent most of their honeymoon sequestered at their remote cabin in the mountains, Caleb had insisted on moving back to town when she got close to term. It hadn't occurred to her to argue.

She looked out on the gorgeous autumn day. The sky was bright blue, without even a wisp of fog, and the bay sparkled in the sunlight. Yet she felt as prickly as a cat before a storm.

Where was Caleb? She looked at her watch. Almost one-thirty. Wasn't his testimony supposed to be over by lunchtime?

Restless, she went back inside. She picked up a dishrag in the kitchen and wiped the counter. Not that there was anything to wipe up. She'd already cleaned the kitchen twice since breakfast. With the baby two weeks overdue and her stomach so huge, she felt more comfortable moving around.

The baby kicked, giving her a jolt.

Shannon touched her belly gently. "I'm as eager to play as you are, little one, so anytime you decide to make an appearance—"

The phone rang.

"It has to be Caleb." She waddled over to answer it. "Hello?"

"Hi, Shannon, it's Sid. Caleb back from court yet?"

"No, he's not, Sid." She glanced at the clock again. "But he should be here soon."

"How that scum Knox could plead not guilty is beyond me," the agent said. "Your testimony alone should've been enough to put him away for life."

A chill ran through her. Malcolm Knox was her least-favorite subject. Unfortunately, until the trial was over and he was behind bars—

"They'll put him away," Sid said, interrupting her thoughts.

"I'm sure they will," she said. They had to. She couldn't stand the idea of Knox tainting their lives any longer.

"You don't sound too well, *chica*. Are you sure you're okay?"

"I'm fine, Sid." Or she would be when Caleb got here. "I'll have Caleb call you."

Minutes after she hung up, the phone rang again. She picked up the bedroom extension. This time it was Brandon asking for Caleb. It had taken months for her husband's partner to return to normal. Even so, the doctor had ordered that he not be allowed to return to his job.

"Sorry, Brandon, I'll have to have him call you."

"That's okay," Brandon said. "Hey, did Caleb tell you our news?"

A twinge in her lower back had her reaching back to rub away the ache. "What news?" she asked distractedly.

"Um, never mind, just have him call, will you?" He hung up.

Shannon frowned at the phone. "That was strange."

But then everything seemed strange the past few days. She paced, feeling restless. What if something had gone wrong at the trial? What if Knox had been set free?

She sat down on a chair, and her gaze came to rest on their wedding portrait on the wall above their bed. The love they'd felt that day had increased tenfold during the eight months they'd been married. If anything happened now...

As if she willed it, Caleb walked into the room.

A more beautiful sight she'd never seen.

She pushed herself awkwardly out of the chair.

Caleb rushed over to help her. Immediately she went into his arms. "I was so worried."

"You shouldn't have been." He tilted up her chin. "Are you all right? You look a little pale."

She smiled. "And you look wonderful."

Bruised and beaten and injured, he'd been devastating enough. Without all the extras, he was the most gorgeous specimen of manhood she'd ever seen. And he was all hers.

"Shannon? Are you sure you're okay?"

She nodded. "I've just been a little restless today. How did the trial go?"

"Guilty on all counts," he told his wife, happy to be able to give her good news. "The jury was back within the half hour. Knox will never see freedom again."

Shannon searched his face. "There's more, isn't there?"

Caleb slipped out of his suit jacket. "He still refuses to give up the names of the creeps he was working for. He says he feels safer keeping the information to himself."

"But why?" Shannon asked. "That was why he wanted the marked money, so he could set them up."

Caleb had wondered the same thing. "I suspect he's planning a little blackmail."

The phone rang. Caleb grabbed it. "Carlisle."

"Gallagher's awake."

"He is?" Sean Gallagher had been in a coma the past few months, with the doctors holding out no hope for his recovery. Caleb tried not to care, but he did.

"And he's talking," Sid added.

Caleb frowned at the way his friend said it. "Talking about what?"

"Seems the captain did some investigation of Knox, trying to come up with something to get him off the hook. It seems Knox had an apartment no one knew about. We searched it this morning."

"And found?" Caleb prompted.

"Everything! Names, dates, cash, drugs." Sid laughed. "We got 'em, Caleb. We got the big guys."

Caleb laughed with him. "That's great, buddy."

"Well, gotta go. We got lots of work to do," his friend said. "I'll talk to you later."

Caleb hung up, then repeated the conversation to Shannon.

"Oh, Caleb, that's wonderful."

Drawn by the beauty of her smile, Caleb walked over to his wife. Even nine-plus months pregnant, Shannon was the sexiest woman he'd ever seen.

He pulled her into his arms. "*You're* wonderful," he said, then kissed her.

Her mouth opened for him, welcoming him with a warmth that ignited a fire in his belly. "I want you." Pushing his hands under her loose top, he ran them over the soft skin of her back, pulling her as close as her swollen belly would allow. Her breasts pressed against his chest, burning twin holes of desire. Unable to resist, he gently teased her nipples with his thumbs.

Shannon moaned and bit into the side of his neck. "Caleb, Caleb, how can you want me when I'm so big and clumsy?"

He smiled down at her. "How could you want me when I looked as if I'd been through a meat grinder?"

Her green gaze misted over like a forest in the rain. "How could I not want you? You were so big and tough-looking." She ran a finger down his cheek. "Yet when you flashed that dimple at me, I was lost."

"I felt the same about your eyes," he told her. "They were so green, so shadowed with secrets, yet when you looked at me, I felt like I was drowning in them."

She pulled his head down and captured his mouth. They kissed again and again, moving by silent consent toward the bed.

Caleb gently lowered her onto the quilt.

Shannon's eyes widened, and she drew in a sharp breath.

Caleb jumped back. "What? Did I hurt you?"

She shook her head. "Help me up."

Heart racing with fear, he did as she asked, being careful not to jolt her. "Honey, what's wrong? Did I move you the wrong way?"

"Caleb…"

He studied her closely. She was breathing harshly, as if she'd been running.

And it hit him. "You're in labor."

She grabbed his hand and squeezed. "No kidding."

"What do I do?" As a rookie cop, he'd seen three babies delivered. But they weren't *his* baby. He was at a loss.

"Caleb," Shannon said sweetly, "take me to the hospital."

FIFTEEN MINUTES LATER they were in a birthing suite at the hospital. The room was dimly lit and pleasantly decorated with flowered wallpaper and soft colors. It contained a rocking chair just perfect for new parents to sit cuddling their newborn.

Shannon saw none of it.

All she could see was Caleb.

They'd brought the painting that she was supposed to focus on during labor. The nurse had hung it on the wall. But Shannon didn't care.

Caleb was the most beautiful sight she'd ever seen. He was what she focused on as the pains grew stronger and closer together. Her big tough husband hissed and breathed, petted and cajoled, and smiled patiently as she went through the labor that would bring them their precious baby.

Between contractions she kissed his hand. "Caleb, I love you."

He flashed his wonderful dimple at her. "I love you, too, honey."

"I'm sorry I was so hard on you."

He raised a dark eyebrow. "What are you talking about?"

"I was so afraid of losing you." It still scared her that his job was so dangerous. "I didn't want to be hurt again. But I wouldn't have changed this for the world."

Another contraction took over, sending her into oblivion. When it eased, she closed her eyes and lay quietly for a moment.

A nurse came into the room to examine her.

"How much longer is this going to take?" Caleb asked. "She's exhausted."

"Not too long now," the nurse said patiently.

Caleb scowled. "That's what you said last time."

The nurse shrugged and smiled. "Babies come in their own time." Then she left the room.

Shannon touched Caleb's arm. "Did you call Zoe?"

His frown disappeared. "First thing. She's on her way."

"Oh, I forgot—Brandon called."

"I talked to him."

She closed her eyes again. Then she remembered. "What was your news?"

"News?"

She opened her eyes and looked at him. His face was drawn and anxious. She reached out to touch his cheek. "Poor guy, this is as hard on you as it is on me."

He kissed her finger. "I don't think so."

"So, tell me the news. Brandon said you had news."

He grinned. "Oh, *that* news. I was going to wait until the baby was born, but..."

She raised a brow. "But...?"

"The reason I was late today was that I went by the office to hand in my resignation."

A contraction threatened. She rubbed her belly. "You're quitting the SDU? But you love your job."

"Not as much as I love you."

The contraction strengthened. "I won't...I can't..." she said between breaths. "Not because...of me...don't have to."

"Relax, honey, quit talking and breathe," he said gently.

He refused to talk until her contraction had leveled off.

Once she could relax again, she gazed into his eyes. "You don't have to."

He grinned. "Then what will I tell the corporate sponsors who've agreed to fund our project?"

"Project?"

"Brandon and I are going to start a program aimed at preventing drug abuse. We'll give lectures to school and businesses, arrange special activities for kids, handle crisis counseling, that kind of stuff."

And he wouldn't be a cop anymore, she thought. He wouldn't be in danger. She looked at him. "Will this make you happy?"

He kissed her. "*You* make me happy."

A sharp contraction hit.

A half hour later, Caitlin Callista Carlisle came screaming into the world.

Proud of both his girls, Caleb gazed into his wife's eyes as she cradled their darling daughter.

"Isn't she terrific, Caleb?"

He had to agree. "You're both terrific."

Shannon's eyes sparkled.

The secrets and shadows were gone. Love for him

and their child glowed with the light of a thousand candles.

Without looking away, he brought her left hand to his lips, kissed the ring that symbolized their union and repeated the words that filled his heart now and forever. "*You* make me happy."

Where the bond of family, tradition and honor run as deep and are as vast as the great Lone Star state, that's...

TRUEBLOOD, TEXAS

Texas families are at the heart of the next Harlequin 12-book continuity series.

HARLEQUIN®
INTRIGUE

is proud to launch this brand-new series of books by some of your very favorite authors.

Look for

SOMEONE S BABY
by Dani Sinclair
On sale May 2001

SECRET BODYGUARD
by B.J. Daniels
On sale June 2001

UNCONDITIONAL SURRENDER
by Joanna Wayne
On sale July 2001

Available at your favorite retail outlet.

USA Today bestselling author

STELLA CAMERON

and popular American Romance author

MURIEL JENSEN

come together in a special
Harlequin 2-in-1 collection.

Look for

Shadows and *Daddy in Demand*

On sale June 2001

HARLEQUIN®
Makes any time special ®

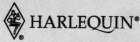

HARLEQUIN WALK DOWN THE AISLE TO MAUI CONTEST 1197
OFFICIAL RULES
NO PURCHASE NECESSARY TO ENTER

1. To enter, follow directions published in the offer to which you are responding. Contest begins April 2, 2001, and ends on October 1, 2001. Method of entry may vary. Mailed entries must be postmarked by October 1, 2001, and received by October 8, 2001.

2. Contest entry may be, at times, presented via the Internet, but will be restricted solely to residents of certain geographic areas that are disclosed on the Web site. To enter via the Internet, if permissible, access the Harlequin Web site (www.eHarlequin.com) and follow the directions displayed online. Online entries must be received by 11:59 p.m. E.S.T. on October 1, 2001.

   In lieu of submitting an entry online, enter by mail by hand-printing (or typing) on an 8½" x 11" plain piece of paper, your name, address (including zip code), Contest number/name and in 250 words or fewer, why winning a Harlequin wedding dress would make your wedding day special. Mail via first-class mail to: Harlequin Walk Down the Aisle Contest 1197, (in the U.S.) P.O. Box 9076, 3010 Walden Avenue, Buffalo, NY 14269-9076, (in Canada) P.O. Box 637, Fort Erie, Ontario L2A 5X3, Canada.

   Limit one entry per person, household address and e-mail address. Online and/or mailed entries received from persons residing in geographic areas in which Internet entry is not permissible will be disqualified.

3. Contests will be judged by a panel of members of the Harlequin editorial, marketing and public relations staff based on the following criteria:

   • Originality and Creativity—50%
   • Emotionally Compelling—25%
   • Sincerity—25%

   In the event of a tie, duplicate prizes will be awarded. Decisions of the judges are final.

4. All entries become the property of Torstar Corp. and will not be returned. No responsibility is assumed for lost, late, illegible, incomplete, inaccurate, nondelivered or misdirected mail or misdirected e-mail, for technical, hardware or software failures of any kind, lost or unavailable network connections, or failed, incomplete, garbled or delayed computer transmission or any human error which may occur in the receipt or processing of the entries in this Contest.

5. Contest open only to residents of the U.S. (except Puerto Rico) and Canada, who are 18 years of age or older, and is void wherever prohibited by law; all applicable laws and regulations apply. Any litigation within the Province of Quebec respecting the conduct or organization of a publicity contest may be submitted to the Régie des alcools, des courses et des jeux for a ruling. Any litigation respecting the awarding of a prize may be submitted to the Régie des alcools, des courses et des jeux only for the purpose of helping the parties reach a settlement. Employees and immediate family members of Torstar Corp. and D. L. Blair, Inc., their affiliates, subsidiaries and all other agencies, entities and persons connected with the use, marketing or conduct of this Contest are not eligible to enter. Taxes on prizes are the sole responsibility of winners. Acceptance of any prize offered constitutes permission to use winner's name, photograph or other likeness for the purposes of advertising, trade and promotion on behalf of Torstar Corp., its affiliates and subsidiaries without further compensation to the winner, unless prohibited by law.

6. Winners will be determined no later than November 15, 2001, and will be notified by mail. Winners will be required to sign and return an Affidavit of Eligibility form within 15 days after winner notification. Noncompliance within that time period may result in disqualification and an alternative winner may be selected. Winners of trip must execute a Release of Liability prior to ticketing and must possess required travel documents (e.g. passport, photo ID) where applicable. Trip must be completed by November 2002. No substitution of prize permitted by winner. Torstar Corp. and D. L. Blair, Inc., their parents, affiliates, and subsidiaries are not responsible for errors in printing or electronic presentation of Contest, entries and/or game pieces. In the event of printing or other errors which may result in unintended prize values or duplication of prizes, all affected game pieces or entries shall be null and void. If for any reason the Internet portion of the Contest is not capable of running as planned, including infection by computer virus, bugs, tampering, unauthorized intervention, fraud, technical failures, or any other causes beyond the control of Torstar Corp. which corrupt or affect the administration, secrecy, fairness, integrity or proper conduct of the Contest, Torstar Corp. reserves the right, at its sole discretion, to disqualify any individual who tampers with the entry process and to cancel, terminate, modify or suspend the Contest or the Internet portion thereof. In the event of a dispute regarding an online entry, the entry will be deemed submitted by the authorized holder of the e-mail account submitted at the time of entry. Authorized account holder is defined as the natural person who is assigned to an e-mail address by an Internet access provider, online service provider or other organization that is responsible for arranging e-mail address for the domain associated with the submitted e-mail address. **Purchase or acceptance of a product offer does not improve your chances of winning.**

7. Prizes: (1) Grand Prize—A Harlequin wedding dress (approximate retail value: $3,500) and a 5-night/6-day honeymoon trip to Maui, HI, including round-trip air transportation provided by Maui Visitors Bureau from Los Angeles International Airport (winner is responsible for transportation to and from Los Angeles International Airport) and a Harlequin Romance Package, including hotel accomodations (double occupancy) at the Hyatt Regency Maui Resort and Spa, dinner for (2) two at Swan Court, a sunset sail on Kiele V and a spa treatment for the winner (approximate retail value: $4,000); (5) Five runner-up prizes of a $1000 gift certificate to selected retail outlets to be determined by Sponsor (retail value $1000 ea.). Prizes consist of only those items listed as part of the prize. Limit one prize per person. All prizes are valued in U.S. currency.

8. For a list of winners (available after December 17, 2001) send a self-addressed, stamped envelope to: Harlequin Walk Down the Aisle Contest 1197 Winners, P.O. Box 4200 Blair, NE 68009-4200 or you may access the www.eHarlequin.com Web site through January 15, 2002.

Contest sponsored by Torstar Corp., P.O. Box 9042, Buffalo, NY 14269-9042, U.S.A.

PHWDACONT2